DATE DUE #3

TYNDALE HOUSE PUBLISHERS, INC., CAROL STREAM, ILLINOIS

Overdrive

CHRIS FABRY

RPM

3

Visit Tyndale's exciting Web site at www.tyndale.com

TYNDALE and Tyndale's quill logo are registered trademarks of Tyndale House Publishers, Inc.

Overdrive

Designed by Stephen Vosloo

Edited by Lorie Popp

Technical consultation by Amber Burger

Library of Congress Cataloging-in-Publication Data

Fabry, Chris, date.
  Overdrive / Chris Fabry.
    p. cm. — (RPM ; #3)
  Summary: As Jamie fights to earn her NASCAR license, her foster brother, Tim, takes a job in the Maxwell garage and finds out more about his father's death.
  ISBN-13: 978-1-4143-1266-8 (softcover : alk. paper)
  ISBN-10: 1-4143-1266-0 (softcover : alk. paper)
  [1. Automobile racing—Fiction. 2. Sex role—Fiction. 3. Foster home care—Fiction. 4. Christian life—Fiction. 5. Family life—North Carolina—Fiction. 6. NASCAR (Association)—Fiction. 7. North Carolina—Fiction.] I. Title.
  PZ7.F1178Ove 2008
  [Fic]—dc22   2007042720

Printed in the United States of America

14 13 12 11 10 09 08
7   6   5   4   3   2   1

This book is dedicated to Colin Fabry,
who provided expert technical assistance
on the subject of diabetes.
I'm proud of you.

"The winner ain't the one with the fastest car. It's the one who refuses to lose."

Dale Earnhardt

"Auto racing is boring except when a car is going at least 172 miles per hour upside down."

Dave Barry

"There are only three sports: bullfighting, motor racing, and mountaineering; all the rest are merely games."

Ernest Hemingway

THE RACE WAS nearing the start when the woman returned to the stands with the young girl. "Come on. We're going to miss it."

"Sorry, Mom," Jenna said. "Can we get something to drink?"

"That'll just make you go to the bathroom again. Let's go."

The two wore #14 shirts and hats, as did the man at their seats, who welcomed them. He gave Jenna a drink of his Coca-Cola as the pace car pulled out. In the sea of people, these three were simply specks.

The man leaned over, and the woman pulled out one earplug. "I just heard Maxwell is having spotter trouble."

"What's wrong?" she said, then dipped her head to hear him over the engine roar.

Prologue

"Not sure, but there's somebody new up there."

The woman stared vacantly at the track, and lines of worry formed on her forehead.

"You okay?" the man said.

"It's Jenna. She's going to the bathroom constantly. And she's not faking it. She really has to go."

"Maybe it's an infection," the man said, looking past his wife at his daughter. Jenna wore headphones, tuned to Dale Maxwell's channel. "She's lost a lot of weight, and she didn't have much to lose to begin with."

"I can't get her to eat much of anything," the woman said. "She used to dream of corn dogs and mustard but not anymore. Only thing she likes is eggs."

The man leaned over and pulled a chocolate bar from the cooler. "Jenna, you want some?"

Her face was pale and her eyes droopy. Her skin clung to her cheekbones and she looked tired. No energy. "No, Daddy. I'm not hungry. Besides, that hurts my tummy."

The dad stood and stared at the race as the pace car veered away and the cars approached the start line. The crowd rose, and the cheering almost drowned out the noise of the engines. Almost. But the noise couldn't drown out the worry etched on the man's face.

The man focused his binoculars on the Maxwell war wagon and Maxwell's crew chief, T.J. Kelly, sitting at the helm.

The woman stood and leaned close. "She's talked about this day for months. Her first Daytona."

"It was so cute how she saved her allowance money for souvenirs," he said. "We have to get her into the doctor this week."

"Tomorrow," the woman said. "I'll take her tomorrow."

Jenna sat back and put her head on the back of the seat.

The man traded seats with his wife and leaned down to Jenna. "You want me to hold you on my shoulders? You'll be able to see better."

Her face told the story. She shook her head and winced, putting a hand on her stomach. "I don't feel good."

He patted her head. "It's all right, pumpkin. Just rest." He turned back to his wife. "Something's definitely wrong."

The woman nodded. "I'll call the doctor first thing in the morning, and we'll get her in for a checkup."

The race took on a life of its own as the husband and wife watched Dale Maxwell move from the middle of the pack. A girl named Jamie was the spotter.

The woman turned to the man. "Doesn't Dale have a daughter named Jamie? Could that be his daughter?"

She spoke as if she knew the family—and she did,

from afar, of course, just like the rest of the fans. She had followed Maxwell for years and appreciated his character, his clean driving, and the fact that he put family and faith first.

When the first caution came out, the woman leaned over to see if her daughter had seen the accident. She touched Jenna, but the girl didn't stir.

"Honey, she's not responding!" the woman yelled.

"Jenna!" the man said.

If the two had been at church or a baseball game or a hundred other places, they would have disturbed the people around them, but not here. Few noticed the man picking up the young girl and hurrying to the paramedics. No one in the crowd of more than 160,000 glanced at the ambulance as it pulled away from the venue with the woman in the back with the girl, rubbing her arms and speaking comforting words while the EMTs put an IV in her arm.

Nor did they see the man running to the parking lot, searching for his car, turning one way, then another, tears streaming. He stopped at a line of portable bathrooms, pulled out his cell phone, and dialed. His face strained, his body shaking, he leaned against a chain-link fence.

"Pastor, there's something wrong with Jenna. I need you to pray."

JAMIE MAXWELL'S MOUTH fell open, and she stared at Bud Watkins, the grizzled old guy in charge of the driving school. She couldn't believe what he had just said. After coming up with the money for the school and setting her heart on finishing, he'd told her to pack her bags and leave.

As far as she knew, she hadn't broken any of the rules. She hadn't smoked, rubbed snuff, consumed alcohol, or done any other prohibited things. She hadn't even eaten the calorie-filled pizza at the restaurant in the lobby of the hotel.

"Just go on back to your room and I'll call your parents to come take you home," Bud said.

Chapter 1
The Test

Jamie's mind spun as she grabbed the doorknob. She wanted to cry. She wanted to scream. She wanted to run from this place and never come back. But something stopped her. She let go of the knob, the door opening.

"Go on," Bud said. "Get out of here."

Jamie turned back to him. "I know you're the king of this place and you have the power to send me home anytime you want. I'm okay with that. But I sold my race car to come here, and I put my future in your hands. Now you take all that away—plus the chance to realize a dream—"

"What are you saying?" Bud said, his face pained.

She took a breath. "I'm saying that I at least deserve an explanation. Why are you kicking me out?" Her voice was strained and her face felt flushed. She was sure there were veins sticking out of her neck. "I've done everything you asked. And all I want is to be treated fairly."

Bud looked hard at her and bit his lower lip.

When he didn't say anything, Jamie shook her head. "So why am I being kicked out?"

He put on his white Stetson and stood, waving a hand. "All right, you passed. Go back to the hotel."

Jamie squinted like she hadn't heard him correctly. "Say that again. I passed what?"

He shoved his car keys in his pocket. "If you read

the fine print of the contract, you'll see that there is a bunch of tests—and not just on the track. Some people here are too timid. Good drivers but they don't stand up for themselves."

"And that was the rap against me?"

"That's the rap against your old man. Nice guy. Works hard. But he lets others push him around."

"Like Devalon," she said.

"Yep."

Jamie blew out a breath. "And if I'd have walked out of here, you would have let me. Game over, just like that."

"Listen, Jamie. You gotta *want* what's here. We're not giving it away. You have to reach out and take it. If you're willing to walk away without a fight, that only proves what people say is true."

Jamie narrowed her eyes at him. "I'm going to be the first woman to win the cup, and my dad isn't a pushover."

Bud shrugged.

"And the name's Maxwell. You call all the guys by their last names. I expect the same for me."

He stared at her. "Fair enough, Maxwell. You should know that we're extending the school into July. The board made the decision last night."

"But won't that be hard—I mean, I don't think I have enough money for room and board."

"The extra time is being covered. That is, if you want to keep learning."

Jamie nodded. "I want that license. I'll be here."

She almost slammed the door behind her, but she didn't want to go too far. Now she knew what to expect—and that was just about anything.

She jogged back to the hotel, feeling 10 pounds lighter and ready to drive again.

TIM CARHARDT SAT in the bank security office thinking he had royally messed up his chances at a new life. He was sure the police would come and take him away and he'd get sent to a reform school in Florida. He had stolen a key from a letter addressed to his distant cousin Tyson Slade. That was his crime—he was trying to look at what was inside a safe-deposit box at this North Carolina bank. But the bank had stopped the whole process and made him sit here.

The security guard (his shirt pocket said *Stout*) sat on the edge of the desk, his arms crossed like a gargoyle on one of those old castles in a horror movie.

"I didn't do anything wrong," Tim said. "That's my dad's stuff in the box."

Mr. Stout didn't say anything, but when Tim got up, he blocked his exit and Tim just rolled his eyes and sat again.

A guy in a suit approached the room along with Mrs. Maxwell, a worried look on her face. She asked questions and interrupted the guy, then dialed her cell phone.

Great, Tim thought. *Now she's calling Dale. Or maybe she's calling for a bus to ship me out of here.*

Tim hated the fact that he'd let the Maxwells down. He hated that he'd caused them trouble. He wanted to crawl away somewhere and die, like an old dog.

Kellen, the youngest Maxwell, walked up to the door and pressed his nose against the glass, cupping his hands around his eyes so he could see inside. He smiled and waved when he saw Tim.

Tim nodded, then looked at the floor. He felt like a criminal, and the voices of Tyson Slade and his wife, Vera, returned. "What would your daddy think?" Vera had said when he'd busted the mailbox of a neighbor.

The door finally opened and Mrs. Maxwell entered. The guard left and closed the door, with Kellen still outside.

"You okay?" she said.

He nodded, looking away.

"We were worried when you didn't come back."

"Got tied up here. I thought I could make it in time, but it took me a while to find the place, and then they kept me here."

"You want to tell me about it?" Mrs. Maxwell said.

"Not much to tell. Tyson got a letter with a key in it, and it said some of my dad's stuff was in a box here. I just wanted to see what was in it."

"Does Tyson know you have the key?" she said.

Tim shook his head. "I kind of intercepted it."

Mrs. Maxwell's cell phone vibrated, and she stepped outside.

Tim looked out the window toward the street and imagined squeezing through and running down an alley. He'd let his mind go like that in stressful situations—especially in school in Florida. The teacher would talk about some complicated problem or people would tease him about sitting at the back of the class, and he'd close his eyes and tear an engine apart or ride with his dad or go through prerace motions at a track. He could spend an hour going through those memories or following the initial spark of the engine switches all the way through the process of making a car come to life.

"Tim?"

At that moment he was scaling a brick wall at the back of an alley, trying to find a way over. He opened his eyes and saw Mrs. Maxwell.

"How are you doing?" she said.

He stood. "Yeah, I'm fine."

The bank guy with the suit was behind her. "Mrs. Maxwell has explained everything and you're free to go. I'm sorry to hear about your father."

Tim's eyes darted between the two of them. He wanted to ask about the key and the box, but he figured getting out of here was enough right now.

The security guy, Stout, stood back with his arms at his sides. When Tim passed, he nodded, as if he was trying to say, *Sorry about all that happened to you, buddy.*

Kellen ran up to Tim as they left the bank. "I'll show you where we parked."

JAMIE LOVED RACING XBOX and PlayStation video games, but the race simulator (known as the RS 43) was more advanced than anything she'd ever played. The RS would let her choose any track in the country that featured cup races and some that didn't. Charlotte looked and felt like Charlotte. Talladega and Daytona were the favorite choices of just about all the students because there were no restrictor plates here—on the straightaway, Jamie had gone 234.

This morning she chose Pocono because that was her dad's next race. She punched in the right series of numbers and watched the familiar tri-oval, 2.5-mile track appear on the screen. There was the tunnel. The short shoot. The front stretch. And, of course, the long pond. It was one of the oddest-shaped tracks in NASCAR but one of her favorites. She loved looking at the surrounding woods and snow fences.

Jamie loved going to Pocono with the family. It was usually right after school let out, and she and Kellen and her mom would drive through Virginia, Maryland, and into Pennsylvania. It was a gorgeous trip with all the trees and flowers so green, and since their dad was usually already there, they'd stretch the nine-hour drive into two days of shopping (which irritated Kellen). They'd find quaint shops along the way and an outlet mall or two, then spend the night at some lodge with moose heads on the walls.

Kellen always insisted on naming the heads and said hello as they went through the lobby. "See you, Billy Bob," he'd say. "Have a good night, Beauregard."

The front desk workers smiled, which only made it worse.

Now, sitting in the simulator, the Pocono track laid out in front of her, she couldn't help smiling too. She missed her family. She missed home, though she didn't miss the last days of school. She had finished all those tests and assignments like she'd promised, and her senior year was staring her in the face, but that seemed like a million years away with the summer just beginning.

She chose the test-drive function of the simulator

and drove out of the pits, shifting through the gears and getting up to speed. She took it easy the first time around, then hit the accelerator as she turned onto the front stretch and passed the start line. You could really get the speed up on this mile-long stretch, but if you didn't slow down for turn one, you were toast.

Jamie drove two laps before checking her best lap times against the other drivers in the school. She was fourth at the moment, but her competitive juices made her start again, and she didn't stop until her initials were at the top of the list.

When she went into race mode, racing against the familiar cars of current drivers, things were a lot different. She had to maneuver to the directions of an electronic spotter who told her when she was clear. Every now and then, something would happen with the simulator that surprised her. A deer would jump onto the track or a spectator with her name painted on his chest would climb to the top of the flag stand and wave. The simulator tried to make drivers concentrate on everything but the race, and she had driven long enough to know that she had to narrow her focus to a pinpoint and keep it there the whole race.

But the simulator didn't just gauge how fast you could go or how many cars you could pass. It also studied reflexes of a crash ahead, how fast you noticed a rising temperature needle or a needed wedge adjustment, whether you could drive the correct speed in the pit areas, and more. Bud and the other teachers received printouts of each session, so there was no playing around. If they caught you burning the tires or driving through the infield, you were gone. That had happened early on to a couple of the guys who thought the RS 43 was a toy. In fact, most students had already been cut.

"This is how it goes in a race," Bud had said. "Just like life. You look around after a few laps, and some cars are back at the garage. It'll be the same here."

Of all the NASCAR tracks on the simulator, the one Jamie returned to each session was Denver. They called it the Mile-High Double Mile because the track was just over two miles, and Denver was at 5,280 feet above sea level. The track wasn't very old, but it had already been the sight of some great races. She loved the mountains in the distance, the extreme banking that was even steeper than Daytona or Talladega, and the thin air. She dreamed about racing there one day.

In her qualifying heats, she had come close to the real track record of just over 201 mph. That made her feel like she could hang in with the best drivers.

When her session was over, she checked her times against the other class members and saw she was slightly ahead of someone with the initials *C.D.* She went through the list of people and couldn't remember anyone with those initials, then climbed out of the simulator to let the next person in.

Kurt Shibley, a cute guy without the swagger and the attitude of some others, was waiting. "How'd you do today?"

"Blistering at Bristol," she said. "Still need some work on the turns at Darlington."

"Sonoma has me bamboozled," Kurt said.

"Oh, Watkins Glen—don't even talk about it." Jamie laughed. "Hey, do you know anybody with the initials *C.D.*?"

Kurt shook his head.

"You two gonna gab all day or are you going to race?" Bud said. "Get to the gym, Maxwell. Trainer's waiting. And you step inside the cockpit, Shibley."

Kurt nodded to Jamie. "I'll check on those initials. Want to talk over dinner?"

"Deal."

ON THE DAY SCHOOL ENDED Tim was cleaning out his locker when Cassie Strower, Jamie's best friend, caught up to him in the hallway. Cassie was pretty but not in a drop-dead gorgeous, cheerleader, and makeup kind of way. She had a great smile and a clean, fresh look that made Tim feel like he needed to take a bath every time he saw her. She had shoulder-length hair that she kept pulling behind one ear.

"Missed you at youth group last week," Cassie said, dipping her head and smiling. She had white teeth too. Looked like she'd never had a cavity in her life.

"Yeah, I kind of got hung up last Wednesday."

"What happened?"

Tim crumpled some papers in the bottom of the locker—tests with lots of red ink on them. "Nothing. Just trying to clear the decks of some junky stuff from my past."

"Really? Like what? I'm interested."

He tossed the crumpled mass toward a trash can, and it bounced off the rim. So much for trying to impress a girl. "There's something of my dad's at this bank, and when I tried to see what it was, they told me I couldn't."

"That's awful," Cassie said. "Can't the Maxwells help you?"

"They tried, but basically Mr. Maxwell said I need to talk with the guy down in Florida I used to live with, and I'm not going for that. Mr. Maxwell talked with the bank and some lawyer guy, I guess."

"What do you think is in the box?"

"I don't have any idea," Tim said. "Maybe I'll never know."

"Well, it's something we can pray about."

Tim found a textbook wedged in the back of the locker. "I don't think God cares much about a kid who steals stuff. Know what I mean?"

Cassie bit her lower lip, and her eyes seemed to bore right through him. "There's a verse in the Psalms that's one of my favorites. It says, 'The Lord is close to the brokenhearted; he rescues those whose spirits are crushed.' Not that I think you're crushed or anything, but I can tell losing your dad really hurt. I've been praying for you."

Tim just stared at her like a deer on a Ferris wheel, wondering what to do or say. She had no idea what had happened to him at churches—the good and the bad. She had no idea how much he hurt every night thinking about his dad. Living at the Maxwells' house made it easier in some ways but harder in others. Harder because as much as they were good to him, he knew he didn't really belong.

He slammed his locker. "Thanks." It was all he could think of to say.

"Have you heard anything from Jamie lately?" Cassie said.

Another sore subject. Tim felt like a fifth wheel near girls in general, and with Jamie he was wheels five and six. "She's still at that driving school and doing okay. Her mom said if everything goes well she'll be there until the middle of July when they have the last race." He paused. "Look—I need to get this book back to my English teacher."

"Sure. See you tonight?"

Tim shrugged and walked away.

AFTER ANOTHER WORKOUT with the trainer, who was more like a drill sergeant, Jamie felt good but exhausted. She showered and dressed, then had a light lunch and headed to the afternoon meeting in the video room. Each day was different, with some people going to the track and some to the simulators. Her individual media training was coming up, and Jamie dreaded it. The camera scared her more than a line of cars trying to pass her on the backstretch at Brickyard. Some had already gone through the training, and one had been sent home afterward.

On the way to dinner Jamie phoned her mother and told her all she'd been through that day. Funny how she never felt like talking with her mom when she was in the house, but when she was away, she enjoyed it, even looked forward to it.

Chapter 5

C.D.

"How's Tim?" Jamie said.

Her mother sighed. "We're kind of at a loss for what to do. He won't talk about what he did, and your dad insists we not take care of it for him. He wants Tim to work it out himself."

"But he's only a high schooler," Jamie said.

"True, but your dad thinks it's best and I agree."

"Sounds like a tough situation for everybody."

"Tim's really good with Kellen, and your dad says he shows a lot of promise in the garage. Now that school is out . . . well, we'll see what happens."

Jamie reached the dining room of the restaurant, and Kurt waved at her. "Gotta go. I'm having dinner with a friend."

"Is he cute?"

Jamie laughed. "Bye, Mom."

Kurt was sitting with Rosa Romero, another student who had welcomed Jamie and seemed nice.

Jamie went through the buffet line and picked out her food, then sat with the two.

"Hear about the new guy?" Rosa said.

"New guy?" Jamie said. "How could there be a new guy?"

Rosa shook her head. "Somebody with money must have pulled a few strings, because he's here. He was in the simulators last night, trying stuff out. He should be in class tomorrow."

"But they've already sent home a bunch of kids," Jamie said. "That's not fair."

"All's fair in love and racing," Kurt said in his best Bud Watkins impersonation. "You know that, little missy."

Jamie couldn't help but laugh. "I almost got sent home because they thought I wasn't tough enough. How can they let somebody come in after we've been here so long?"

"It doesn't matter," Rosa said. "We have to keep our heads and work to get through this."

"That's why we wanted to talk to you," Kurt said.

"You mean this isn't just friendly dinner conversation?" Jamie felt a little hurt but smiled to hide it.

Kurt wolfed some hamburger and leaned closer. "Everybody here is racing for themselves, trying to get those coveted licenses. But you know that's not the way they do it in the big show. They have teammates. The team works together on the track."

"What are you saying?" Jamie said.

Kurt wiped his mouth with a napkin. "The sooner we make an alliance with like-minded people, the better off we'll be. We don't have to announce it to anybody, but before we get to the track, it'll be good to know there are other people out there blocking for us, giving us a chance to lead a few laps, that kind of thing."

"Makes sense," Jamie said. "But the others could figure it out. And what if Bud—?"

"There's nothing illegal about what we're doing," Rosa said. "In fact, it'll probably impress the instructors that we're working together."

Jamie nodded. "But there's no guarantee we'll be on the track together. They could catch on and put us in different heats."

"Then we bring on others we can trust." Kurt looked around. "You've seen the hotshots here. The ones with the swagger that think they'll win the cup next year if they can just get a license and get signed on by one of the big racing teams."

Jamie stuck out a hand. Kurt shook it; then Rosa did.

"It's a deal, then," Jamie said. "We'll watch each other's backs as much as possible."

Someone approached the table behind Jamie, and Kurt and Rosa looked up.

"Well, this looks like a mighty friendly table," a familiar voice said.

Jamie turned. The guy had on a black jacket and flashed a million-dollar smile at her. Every hair was in place as he glided toward the table and held out a bottle.

"Brought you some Yoo-hoo," Chad Devalon said.

TIM SAT CROSS-LEGGED and hunched over lawn mower parts strewn about the driveway in front of the Maxwells' garage. Everyone in the family had chores, and Kellen had dibs on mowing the front lawn. The back lawn was more like a field, and Dale did that with a tractor and a brush hog. Tim took out the trash, cleaned up after the dog, Petty, and did other odds and ends Mrs. Maxwell assigned him. He wasn't thrilled about all the work, but it kept him busy. He was here because Kellen couldn't get the mower started, and one thing led to another and Tim had the whole thing apart.

A shadow crossed the driveway, and Tim could tell by the size of it who it was.

"It's dinnertime. Why don't you come on in?" Dale said.

Chapter 6
Not Even the Sky

"I'm kind of in the middle of this. If it's all right, I'd like to finish."

"I know what it feels like to start something and want to get it back together." Dale knelt and looked at the parts. "What do you think's the problem?"

"Well, I know it's not the gas because the tank is full. I checked that first in case you thought I was numb in the head."

Dale chuckled. "I've done that before."

"Then I pulled off the fuel filter and gave it a good cleaning, and I checked the line, but it's clear. Air filter was a little dirty, but I cleaned that too."

"You check the plug?"

"That's what I looked at next. Found a new one in the garage and put it in. Hope you don't mind."

"Was the old one scuzzy looking?"

"Yeah, it probably still had a little fire to it, but I figured a new one would light it up, but no go. So my next move was—"

"Carburetor," Dale said.

Tim nodded. "You drain the gas tank last winter?"

"No, but it's been running all spring."

"I've seen them run and then get gummed up."

"How do you know so much about engines?" Dale said.

"My dad taught me a thing or two. Plus, I hung

around with some of the guys in the garage. Kind of comes naturally."

Dale retrieved a can of cleaner from the garage, and Tim put the mower back together.

Mrs. Maxwell called to them, but Dale told her they'd be a few more minutes. "Want to see if he gets this thing cranking."

Tim adjusted the screws for the air and gas mixture and stood. "Why don't you give it a pull?"

"No way," Dale said. "You do it."

Tim yanked the rope and the engine coughed. He adjusted the choke a little as Kellen walked out. One more pull and the thing fired and started.

Dale whooped and clapped, and Kellen high-fived Tim.

"You can mow after dinner," Dale said to Kellen. "Go on in and tell your mom we're gonna clean up."

Kellen went into the house, and Dale handed Tim some Goop to clean his hands. He leaned against a workbench in their home garage and got the grime off, then wiped his hands on a towel.

"We need to talk about a couple of things, and the first is the safe-deposit box," Dale said. "That letter you took was addressed to somebody else. You can't do that. It would be like you opening our mail."

"I'd never do that."

"I know you wouldn't. But you understand that was wrong."

"Yes, sir."

"Don't hang your head like a whipped puppy. I'm not coming down on you. I can understand why you'd do it, and I can't say that I blame you."

"I guess there was probably a better way to do it," Tim said.

Dale nodded. "Like it or not, Tyson has control of that box. You want to see it, he has to give permission."

"I can't talk to him again," Tim said. "I'd rather swim across that big lake out there with milk jugs tied to my ankles."

Dale looked like he was trying not to smile. "I understand. Again, I don't blame you. But I have to ask something. You want to know what's in that box?"

Tim nodded.

Dale put up both hands. "There you go." He came over to Tim and stood beside him, shoulder to shoulder. "Sometimes we let people get big. They get this choke hold on us, and we let them get bigger and bigger because we don't stand up to them."

"You talking about Tyson or that Devalon guy?"

Tim said. "He sure seems to have a choke hold on your driving."

Dale rubbed his face and glanced sideways at Tim. "Let's keep this about you for now."

"Fair enough."

"I've talked with my lawyer, and he says you could go to court and try to get access. He doesn't think that's a good idea. It would cost a lot of money, and you'd probably lose. For whatever reason, your dad appointed Tyson as the executor of his estate. My lawyer says the best thing is to talk to Tyson. Convince him you want to see what's in there."

"Sounds easy for a lawyer to say. He didn't have to live with the guy and his wife."

"I didn't say it would be easy. But I think this is the best approach. Sometimes you have to face the things that scare you the most."

Tim stared at the floor. There was sawdust down there from some woodworking project Kellen had begun. He put the toe of his shoe in it and pushed it around, making a face in the dust.

Dale leaned back against the wall. "This is the last piece of the puzzle with your father. Closes the loop. What do you think?"

"I guess if it's the only way, I can talk to him. Maybe I'll stay here tonight and call him while you guys go to church."

Dale hesitated. "Okay. Sounds like a plan."

"What's the other thing you want to talk about?" Tim said.

Dale turned and stretched. He had strong forearms, and Tim could tell he worked out a lot. Maybe not at a gym like some of the drivers but around the farm. Lifting stuff. Running in the backyard with Kellen.

"I want you to think about something. I believe God gives every one of us some kind of gift to use for his glory. A desire he plants deep down inside. Something you long for, that's on your mind when you wake up in the morning and when you go to sleep at night. Sometimes it feels like you can taste it. You know what I'm talking about?"

Tim shrugged. "I've always dreamed of being a driver."

"That's what I went after when I was your age. You drive much?"

"Little go-karts but I wasn't very good. Do you think a kid who can't drive a go-kart could race a big car?"

Dale laughed. "Sure. But there's something I see in you, that I've noticed over the past few weeks, that makes me think God's pushing you in another direction."

"What's that?"

Dale moved to the garage door and pointed at the lawn mower. "Do you know how many people could diagnose an engine problem like you did— walk through all the steps and tear it apart, then put it back together? And I don't mean kids your age. I mean grown men. They'd get frustrated and take it to a mechanic in no time flat."

"Wasn't nothing special," Tim said.

"That's where you're wrong. It *is* special. And if you apply yourself and learn, you could have what it takes to be on a team."

"A racing team?"

"That's right. And if you're game, I'm thinking of giving you a position at the garage. It won't be anything fancy. You'll have to sweep up and do a lot of gofer work to start. But the guys there can teach you things and help you develop your gift. Who knows where it could take you. Some of the best crew chiefs in—"

"Crew chief? Is that what you think I should be?"

"Some of the best crew chiefs got their start by knowing the ins and outs of the engine. They can listen to a car and tell whether or not it's going to finish strong. They know they can't drive, but they're even-keeled enough to take the heat of the war wagon. They're good with people, they're not full of themselves, and they know that everybody contributes—

not just the driver and the pit crew but *everybody* who works on that team. Yeah, I think you'd be a great mechanic. You'd be a great crew chief someday. But you have to work on it and keep learning every aspect of the car."

Tim looked out at the lawn mower, and something inside clicked. No one had ever talked to him this way—not even his father. His dad had told him he could fix engines and maybe be on a team, but to nail his dreams and give Tim real hope was new. He'd always felt like he'd wind up on life's garbage heap, poking around the edges to find scraps of happiness and fulfillment. But to hear Dale Maxwell, it sounded like he believed Tim could be anything he wanted to be. That not even the sky was the limit to what he could do.

"When could I start at your garage?" Tim said.

JAMIE STARED AT CHAD a few seconds, like a ghost had walked into the room.

Rosa and Kurt obviously knew of him and his dad, because they asked questions and wouldn't stop. Chad just smiled and answered politely, but he didn't take his eyes off Jamie.

Finally Kurt and Rosa said good-bye and left the two of them alone. Jamie didn't know whether to thank them or yell at them to get back to the table.

"What do you think?" Chad said. "Of me being here and all?"

"I think you can't keep a promise," Jamie said.

"What do you mean?"

"Don't you remember what you said back at the Pit Stop? You sat in that booth and told me you'd never be a problem for me again. Never block me or run into me on purpose."

"I never did that anyway," Chad said. "Besides, you take everything personal. It's not—it's just racing."

"So it's my problem and you're innocent of everything."

"You're a good driver. You wouldn't be here if you weren't. But not everything that happens on the track is about you."

Jamie rolled her eyes. "Like you being here, jumping in when the rest of us have worked really hard to stay."

"That has nothing to do with you."

"Can't you see how it makes us feel for them to let you in this far into the session?"

Chad threw up his hands. "Ask *them* that. My dad talked to the people running it, and they thought it would be good for me to mix things up a bit. It's not my fault."

"What about your wreck? I thought your pinched nerve or whatever it was in your neck knocked you out. You could have been killed."

Chad bit into his burger and chewed like Brad Pitt in a nonspeaking scene. "That was a big deal over nothing if you ask me. But I did lose a good car."

Jamie shook her head and tried to calm down. "You've already been on the simulator, haven't you?"

"I got on it late last night and took a few spins to catch up with you guys. Didn't do half bad."

A couple of guys from the school slapped Chad on the back and gave him high fives. Roger and Kenny were both hotshots as far as Jamie was concerned, so she looked the other way while they talked.

"Good to see you up and around," Roger said. He was short with dark, wavy hair and an attitude twice his height.

"I see you know the fastest girl in the school," Kenny said, nodding toward Jamie. He was taller and wore wraparound sunglasses to every class meeting. "Fastest behind the wheel, that is."

"We're old pals from way back," Chad said. Then he added, "She's telling me there's not much competition here."

Jamie's mouth flew open. "That's—I never said anything like that!"

"That's okay," Roger said. "Bud said we're getting some seat time on the track tomorrow." He leaned close to Jamie. "I'm thinking you'll get plenty of time to look at my spoiler."

Jamie laughed, but when the two were gone, she fumed at Chad. "Why'd you have to do that? I don't want to tick these guys off."

"They're just playing with you," Chad said. "They know how good you are. Probably shaking in their boots because of you. They either want to beat you or ask you out. Maybe both."

Jamie blushed. She couldn't remember Chad ever giving her a true compliment—at least one without all the smarm. Had he changed? Was he just looking for an angle to make her let her guard down so he could push the pedal to the floor and pass her on the inside?

She put aside their differences for a moment and thought about her friend Cassie Strower. Cassie had said that Chad didn't need a new car or a win in his next race but a relationship with God. That seemed far-fetched to Jamie. Chad had said he didn't like going to church and his dad provided everything he needed.

"Let me guess," Jamie said after taking a drink of soda. "Your dad said if you don't come here, he won't fund any more racing for you."

Chad snickered. "You're not just pretty. You got a pretty good head on your shoulders."

"Thanks. I think."

"B.D. knows he holds the purse strings. I can't do much of anything without his say-so."

"You call your dad B.D.?"

"It's a lot better than what my mom calls him." Chad laughed. "He can be just as hard at home as he can be on the track."

"So you're mad at him for sending you here."

"Hey, he just wants what's best, right? 'Honor your father and mother' and all that junk."

Well, he knows at least a little about the Bible, Jamie thought.

"I'll do whatever it takes to get back out there. If it means coming here and finishing on top to prove I'm good enough, I'll do it."

Chad finished his burger, but Jamie picked at her salad. She had gotten used to being out of Chad's shadow—at least for a few weeks—and she liked the feeling. Now she was back in it, and she wasn't sure which she liked more.

TIM SAT ALONE in the Maxwell Motorsports garage, cleaning tools and watching the Chicago race on a wide-screen TV mounted on the wall above an air compressor. It wasn't the fanciest setup he'd ever seen, and the garage was small compared to some teams', but it was still roomy.

He had to hand it to Maxwell—he'd done the whole racing thing his own way, refusing to work for some big owner with a team of drivers who could throw a lot of money at him. There were pictures on the wall of those days when Dale had done his time on other teams, but when he'd established himself as a top-10 driver, he'd struck out on his own. He'd gone from a front-runner with the best equipment money could buy to a middle-of-the-pack racer. He'd kept his

Chapter 8

Deep Dish

reputation and was trying to hang on to his family, but he hadn't won much money. He was the racer a lot of people in the stands cheered for but who knew at the end of the day he'd probably be somewhere other than the winner's circle.

That had changed a bit over the past few races. Dale seemed to shine on the intermediate tracks, and at Michigan he finished in the top 10. New Hampshire brought a #12 finish, and Dale kept the momentum going, racing from back in the pack late in the race at Daytona to capture the seventh slot. He was moving up in points, but the problem was, all of the front-runners were moving up as well. By Chicago, Dale was in 17th place with not a lot of hope at reaching #12 to qualify for the Chase.

As Tim watched the coverage, he remembered one of the times he and his dad had been to Chicago. The race was in July, in the heat of summer, and the year his dad had died they'd been given tickets to a Cubs game at Wrigley Field. They'd gotten a ride from the Joliet cornfields to a train station and rode it the whole way into the belly of the city. His dad had as much trouble following the track changes as he did, and once Tim thought they'd have to turn back, but they finally found the Red Line and got off at Addison, a short walk from the ballpark.

Tim had been to minor league games before

but never to a park like Wrigley, with the ivy on the outfield walls and players so close that it felt like he could reach out and touch them. Babe Ruth had played here, though he didn't know much about him. The bases seemed twice as white and the grass was three times as green as anything he'd ever seen. His dad had told him to hold off on the hot dogs because he had a special dinner planned, so Tim did and his stomach nearly growled louder than the crowd around them when the Cubs won.

They filed out with the other fans and headed back to the train. When they reached downtown, they went underground and his dad looked at a piece of paper he'd scribbled on. They got off the train and walked up the stairs, his dad pointing out a big brick building a block away and saying it was Moody something or other and that some famous preacher started the school. Tim's stomach was past growling and had begun snarling. He followed his dad to a little restaurant with a green awning above it. It had a funny Italian name he couldn't pronounce.

"They say this is the best pizza you'll ever have," his dad said.

"I could eat a horse pizza right now. With a side of porcupine quills."

His dad had laughed, and now Tim wished he

could bottle that sound and open it up any time he felt lonely.

It was dark inside, and the tables all had those red-and-white checkered tablecloths. His dad ordered a pitcher of Coca-Cola and something called a deep-dish pizza, and Tim thought they'd have to order at least two of them to satisfy him. He ate a salad down to the bottom of the bowl while he waited.

When the server brought the pan out still sizzling, Tim couldn't believe his eyes. The thing was a good six inches thick and had all the ingredients he loved stuffed inside it instead of on top. He started to pick it up but decided on cutting it with a fork. The taste of the crust and the sausage and pepperoni and onions and peppers and mushrooms made him want to move to Chicago.

His dad just watched him and smiled. "Something special, isn't it?"

Tim nodded as he cut another piece and put a little of his Thousand Island dressing on the side of the pizza and covered it with Parmesan cheese. The tastes melded together perfectly.

They had two pieces left, and Tim carried the bag home on the train ride, not believing the two pieces he had eaten had filled him to overflowing. The only thing better than that dinner was breakfast the next morning when Tim pulled the bag out of the little refrigerator in his dad's truck and ate both slices. The taste stayed with him all day at the track as they set up for the race.

"You think we could go back to that place sometime?" Tim said.

"Why don't we make it our tradition?" his dad said. "We get one Chicago-style pizza every time we come here."

That memory rushed back, and Tim could almost taste that thick crust as he watched the green flag drop and the grand marshal (who was some famous football player or coach with the Bears) say, "Gentlemen, start your engines."

Dale had qualified in the fifth spot, so he was inside on the third row when they started. The Chicagoland Speedway was one of those places where fuel strategy came into play, and Tim knew that Dale's crew chief, T.J. Kelly, was one of the best.

Early in the race, Dale had trouble getting loose in the turns, especially number three, and he dropped back. After a wreck that took out two of the top contenders happened around lap 40, the crew made an adjustment and Tim could tell the car was handling a lot better.

Before the halfway point, one of the top points leaders, a favorite in the race who had been running at the front almost since the beginning, blew out his right rear tire. The explosion sent rubber flying and spun him around and into the wall. On his way to the infield care center, the driver said, "I thought somebody had dropped a bomb behind me—the explosion was that loud. I figured it was either that or my driveshaft had fallen through. But it was just a tire."

Tim was so engrossed in the race that he didn't realize he'd been cleaning the same air wrench for about 20 laps. It was nice and shiny when he shelved it. He turned and noticed a shadow outside the window. Kind of strange because the place was deserted.

He opened the door and stuck his head out, looking both ways. "Hello? Anybody out here?"

No one was there.

JAMIE SAT IN THE COCKPIT of the #1 RS 43 watching the Chicago race from the pits. The team around her was flying through a four-tire change and refuel. The simulator allowed a student to ride along with her favorite driver or actually race with the field. The only drawback was that there was no digital spotter to talk you through. You were on your own. Jamie chose to ride with her dad and watch his technique rather than race.

Over the weekend, the organizers gave the students a much-needed break and didn't schedule races or activities. Most students had chosen to go home—Chad wasn't around, and Jamie guessed he had flown to Chicago—but some had stayed behind because of lack of funds. Jamie felt she needed to work out some kinks in her passing technique, so she stayed. There were times in her recent races, especially when she found herself in heavy traffic, that she'd head into a turn and slow up too much. It was a mental leap of faith to go more than 150 mph and run up on a car ahead of you and not slow down. Instinct and safety kicked in, and you had to overcome that through seat time and experience.

Jamie had taken a driver's safety course in school because her dad said it was a good idea, and it also saved him money on his car insurance. She had passed easily, but she nearly scared her instructor to death. One day she passed the Velocity Racetrack and saw her dad's hauler outside. The man at the gate let her drive inside because he knew her, and she wound up taking her instructor for a couple of spins around the track. He made her promise that no one would find out about it.

However, somebody did and wrote a letter to the editor of the local newspaper about the incident. The teacher was disciplined, and Jamie felt bad about it.

Fortunately for Jamie, in her kart and racing career, she had spent so much time out in front, in "clean air," that she only had to slow down when she came to lapped traffic. Here at the driving school, it was different. These students were the best of the best, and there were plenty of times when she found herself in midpack or at the back, having to maneuver around several opponents.

"If you're gonna go around a car on the right side, you gotta do it," Bud had said. "Don't just think about it and do the pussyfoot dance." Everyone had laughed at that line. "Mash that sucker to the floor and go. You don't get points for being nice. You're here to win a race."

Jamie had always been known as aggressive and fast on the track. Now she was even more committed to beating the competition.

The Chicago race was half completed when Jamie switched to race mode in the simulator. The machine required her to come out of the pits and merge into race traffic. It was easier, of course, when a yellow flag was out, but even more of a challenge during the green flag.

She watched the leaders approach and pass her, picking up speed and getting into fourth gear. When the #13 car of Butch Devalon screamed past, she got in behind him and hit the third turn and tried to keep up. Since it was a virtual machine, anyone following could drive right through her (a weird feeling to watch another car pass through hers), but as long as she kept pace, she was fine.

Butch was her father's nemesis. He was mean, had a reputation as a dirty driver, and always accused Christians of being Bible-thumpers with no place in the sport. Actually, he was an equal opportunity basher who didn't like anyone winning but himself. He had lots of trophies and money to prove it.

Jamie closed on him down the straightaway, and she looked at her RPM gauge. Unlike real cars, the simulator showed how fast she was going in miles per hour. The speedometer read 193. A blistering pace that she couldn't hold in the turn, so she backed off the accelerator slightly and drove to the right of Devalon.

Remembering Bud's words, she punched the accelerator about halfway through the turn and shot out the other side, hanging on to the steering wheel for all she was worth, then pulled up beside Devalon, who was right up on the steering wheel. Suddenly she caught sight of another car behind them, stealing some air from Devalon. The #13 car slid to the right slightly, and she saw Butch struggle to keep it under control. She mashed the accelerator down just as Devalon lost control. A plume of smoke rose behind her, and a yellow flag flashed at the top of her screen.

"He crashed," Jamie said, mouth open. "Devalon's out of the race!"

TIM WATCHED THE CLEANUP of the Devalon car and shook his head. "Live by the bump draft—die by the bump draft," he muttered.

The door swung open and Kellen ran into the room, full of vinegar (as Tim's dad used to say), which meant he had enough energy for about 50 grown-ups. He was carrying something under his arm and watching the coverage on the screen. "Can you believe Devalon bit it?" he said.

"Bunch of the leaders are gone," Tim said. "If your dad can stay away from the wrecks, he'll move up this week. Whatcha got there?"

"Oh, this was leaning at the front of the building."

Tim took the package, which looked like a shoe box wrapped in brown paper. *Tim Carheart* was written in Magic Marker on the front.

"Who's it from?" Kellen said.

"Nobody who knows how to spell my name." He set the package down on a shelf.

"Aren't you gonna open it?"

"Later," Tim said. "Look, they're coming in to the pits."

"Dad's staying out," Kellen said. "He's gonna take the lead."

"How many points will he get if he wins this?" Tim said.

Kellen told him.

"Do you think he has a shot at the Chase?" Tim said.

"He doesn't talk about it, but I can tell he wants it bad. What with all the trouble his primary sponsor's given him."

"I haven't heard," Tim said. "At least, not the particulars."

Kellen scooted onto a workbench and put his back against the wall. "I don't know everything, but the main sponsor talked about changing the hood to a beer company and dad just about busted a major artery."

"He doesn't like beer?"

"No, he thinks it causes a lot of problems. Doesn't want any little kids seeing him driving around with it on his car and have them think he's okay with it."

"But everybody else does."

Kellen shrugged. "My dad doesn't care what everybody else does."

Tim thought back to his days with Tyson in Florida and wondered what he'd say about Dale. Tyson drank beer like most people drank water. "Maybe all that sponsor trouble will go away if he wins."

The race started again, and it was good to see the #14 car in first place.

"And here's a sight we haven't seen in quite a while," the announcer said. "Dale Maxwell leading a race going into the late stages."

"Dale told me he had a good car out here and he really likes the extra grooves this track has developed over the past few years," a former driver said. "I like his chances a lot because once he gets into clean air, he knows what to do."

The final laps were so thrilling that Tim couldn't concentrate on his work. He moved closer to the screen and couldn't help urging Dale on.

Kellen yelled whenever a challenger came from the back, but every time, Dale held him off with a burst of speed. When the caution came out with 20 laps left, Dale got two right-side tires and a splash of fuel and beat the rest of the field to the line. At the restart, after a furious challenge by Butch Devalon's teammate, Dale surged ahead.

When Dale took the checkered flag, Kellen was jumping up and down and Tim was right next to him, giving him high fives and shouting. Tim couldn't remember being this happy after any race in his life.

"Only thing that would make this better is being there," Tim said.

"Maybe he'll let us go with him to Brickyard," Kellen said.

"That'd be cool."

Dale's exit from his car was understated, unlike a lot of the drivers. Some of them climbed a fence or did a backflip or some other crazy thing that made the news. Dale had told Tim that once you made it to the winner's circle you should act like you've been there before, so he just climbed out, waved at the fans, and smiled.

"It's been a long time since you've been here," the trackside reporter said. "What would you like to say?"

"First, I thank God for giving me the opportunity to be in this sport," Dale said, catching his breath. "I also need to thank my family for their support. My wife and kids and Tim, you guys are my inspiration."

Tim couldn't help getting choked up when he heard his name, but he was really affected when Dale thanked the pit crew for their hard work and attributed the win to them. Then he thanked his sponsors—which was what most drivers usually did first.

"What did you think of that charge at the end to catch you?" the reporter said.

"I knew we had a good car and if I stayed in the groove and didn't let them get too close and get me loose, we were going to win. It's too bad we have next week off. I'd drive this car to Brickyard right now if I could."

Tim laughed and picked up the rest of the tools scattered around the garage. Kellen offered to help him, but Tim said he'd do it himself.

"Okay, see you back at the house," Kellen said.

Tim turned off the TV and arranged the tools the way he'd been told. He couldn't wait until Dale, the crew chief, and the others saw what he'd done. Finally, he picked up the box and unwrapped it. It was a shoe box for an expensive brand of driving shoes. He opened it, expecting to see a pair in there, but he just found some newspaper wrapped around a DVD case. On the front of the DVD were two words written in permanent marker: *October, Talladega*.

A CHILL WENT THROUGH TIM. His
father had died at that Talladega race.
He tossed the box in the big Dumpster
at the back of the building and stuck
the DVD in his pocket. He could have
watched it right here, but he didn't want
to take the chance of somebody walking in on him.

He cleaned up, locked the door, then
searched the gravel parking lot for clues
about who had left the package. How did
they know he was at the garage? Or that
he even worked here? Was it some racing fan or a member of another team?
a friend of his dad's? a friend of Dale's?
Before he jumped to conclusions, he decided to watch the DVD.

One of the mysteries surrounding
his father's death was what actually
happened. There had been a momen-
tary power glitch at the track as Dale

Chapter 11
DVD Truth

Maxwell's car had approached the pits. Maxwell himself had talked to officials and the media, saying he lost control as he came into the area, but there was confusion as to why. Was the entrance slick? Had a tire blown? (Both back tires were flat, but there was no evidence they'd blown.) The official investigation had determined the cause to be a combination of driver error and "track debris," though Tim didn't see it that way. He thought Maxwell was going too fast when he entered pit road, but an official showed him under the limit. There had been talk of discipline of Maxwell, but his reputation as a clean driver and the fact that he had been obeying the speed limit saved him. It was just a freak accident.

NASCAR had done everything they could to make the pit area safer, but the mix of people focused on a task and machines sometimes out of control made it dangerous. All the regulations and precautions in the world couldn't change that.

Tim had drawn up an equation in math class that said:

$$\frac{\textbf{\textit{SPEED + HUMANS}}}{\textbf{\textit{MONEY}}} = \textbf{\textit{TROUBLE}}$$

Tim had seen people take risks and pay the price. He'd also seen people pour their whole lives into winning and become bitter when it didn't happen. The saddest were those who rose to the very top, then realized it was empty up there. He couldn't imagine having all that money and not being happy, but he'd seen it happen.

Tim made his way back to the house just as Mrs. Maxwell was coming outside with her purse over her shoulder. "We're headed to the airport to pick up Dale," she said. "Want to come along?"

"Think I'll stick around here if it's all right with you," Tim said.

"You sure?" Mrs. Maxwell looked at him askance, as if she couldn't believe he didn't want to go or thought maybe he was coming down with a cold.

"Yeah, I want to watch some of the extended coverage," Tim said, flipping on the TV in the front room.

"Okay, we'll have a late dinner when we get back," she said. "Or maybe Dale will want to stop for something at the Pit Stop."

"Sounds good," Tim said. "I'll just grab a sandwich from the fridge."

He sat on the couch while Kellen pulled a cardboard sign down the stairs and taped it to the door. It said Dale Maxwell #1.

Tim caught a couple more interviews of Dale while Mrs. Maxwell and Kellen pulled out of the driveway. When he was sure they were gone, he slipped the

DVD into the player. There was no menu, just one clip that said *3:14*.

Tim took a breath and stood, making sure there was no one outside or that the Maxwells weren't suddenly back, Kellen racing in to retrieve his favorite hat. Then he sat and punched the Play button on the remote.

The camera angle was weird, unlike any on a televised race. It seemed to be from the middle of the infield. Cars screamed around the track, and he lost sight of them in the sea of RVs and TV trucks.

"This is it," Tim whispered.

The camera shook as whoever held it panned left. Cars came into the clear, and just before they reached the exit for the pits, the camera zoomed in on the #14 car slowing and pulling down to the apron.

"No, no, I can't watch this," Tim said, hitting the Pause button. He stood and walked into the kitchen, both hands behind his head, rubbing quickly. It was like watching the grainy video of some presidential assassination or a plane flying into a building. These were the last moments of his father's life. How could he watch that?

How can I not watch?

The fear of watching gave way to a desire for answers. Would the footage show the truth? And why would someone send this DVD? His mind flashed to

Jeff from Florida—a guy who had cheated him out of tickets to Daytona. Could this be his handiwork?

Tim went back to the living room and knelt before the TV. He took a deep breath and hit Play.

The camera quickly pulled back a bit from the #14 car to show the rest of the field. Suddenly, a blur passed and the back of the #14 car lost control. Instead of following it to the pits, the camera showed the blur.

Someone cursed softly, and the camera focused on the pits, where smoke came from Dale Maxwell's car. People scrambled like bees around a hive, and Tim saw his dad's arm sprawled on the race car in front of him, trapped. Two men came to help him, and Dale crawled out of his car, tearing off his helmet, then leaning down to Tim's father. The ambulance and the EMTs came soon after. Tim finally remembered to breathe.

The screen went black, and then another clip started. It showed the Maxwell car in slow motion, but the footage had somehow been enhanced. Frame by frame the blur cleared. Tim leaned closer and squinted until the image stopped.

The car behind Dale Maxwell had clipped him. The frame stopped on the blur until the number came into focus. It was the #13 car.

"Devalon," Tim whispered. "It was you."

JAMIE SAT IN FRONT of a camera in her fire suit, her hair tied in a ponytail, more nervous here than on the track before a big race. The number of students had been cut, and the fine-tuning had begun for the big event—the final race to determine the top tier of racers. One of the things the school promised to address was media skills, and that's where Jamie sat.

The instructor, Charlyn Jacobs, was a petite woman with striking blonde hair, long fingernails, bright red lipstick, and four-inch heels that clacked on the tile floor. All the guys talked about her and made remarks about her makeup and how old she might be (Jamie guessed she was at least 30) and why she didn't wear a wedding ring but had plenty of other jewelry. She had a pretty smile and perfect teeth, but Jamie got the feeling she'd been asked to lead the seminar because behind that pretty facade was a fierce interviewer.

"The job of the media is to get a sound bite from you they can use," Charlyn had said. "I should know. I've covered sports for the past eight years and have been everywhere from the putting greens at Augusta to the Dodgers clubhouse in Los Angeles."

Some guy behind Jamie had snickered and made a smart remark under his breath that got several laughing.

Charlyn stepped forward and put her hands on her hips. "If you want to be the next one to leave the group, keep talking."

The room got quiet.

"This isn't your playtime at kindergarten. This is serious business and will determine how far you can go every bit as much as what happens on the track. So if I were you, I wouldn't honk off a person who has the power to kick your tail out of here and back to some dirt track where you'll be racing the rest of your pathetic life winning $50 or a prize turkey. I can make your life miserable when I get on the other side of the camera. Remember that."

Charlyn didn't have another problem with smart talk. The room had gotten quiet enough to hear mice trimming their nails.

Part of Jamie was scared of her and intimidated:

The other part was happy. Some women in the racing world were treated as trophies. Just pretty things at a driver's side to make him look better. But Charlyn wasn't having any of that. She had a mind of her own and a determination Jamie wanted.

"People judge you by the words you use," Charlyn continued. "And there's a reason that more and more drivers are getting a college education."

She hooked her thumbs in imaginary belt loops, turned a heel to the side, and did her best country-boy pose. "You want to talk like a good ole boy and eat taters and spit off your back porch, go right ahead." She leveled her gaze at them. "That might have worked a few years ago but not anymore. This sport is reaching all over the country to people east, west, and north, not just the South. So clean up your twang. Let everybody—not just your family—understand what you're saying."

Chad raised a hand, and Charlyn nodded to him. "I agree we ought to cut out the *ain't*s and all that, but I've always heard we have to be ourselves. I don't want a college degree. I just want to win."

Charlyn walked past him like she was on the prowl. "Good point. And I do want you to be yourself. The thing that will draw a team to you is the same thing that will draw fans. Something genuine deep down inside. Something they identify with. Something that reminds them that they've been at the back of the pack, believing they can overcome the odds just like you." She stopped right in front of him. "But you need to be the best *you* you can be. If your South Carolina drawl is real, don't get rid of it—use it to your advantage. Words are another tool of the racer, so when you open that mouth, have something to say and don't hem and haw and um and uh."

Jamie knew exactly what Charlyn was talking about. But it was different, of course, when she sat in the interview room facing the camera and the lights. She could see her own face reflected in the camera lens, and she wondered if someday this video would be played during a big race, poking fun at how far Jamie had come. Or would her racing dreams crash right here?

"All right, sit up straight, and let me see that smile of yours. No matter what I throw at you, I want your personality to come through," Charlyn said. "You got it?"

"Got it."

"Ready?"

Jamie scooted back in her seat and took a deep breath. "Ready."

"Why would a nice, pretty girl like you want to ruin an entire sport?"

Jamie's mouth dropped open. "Uh . . . well, I mean, I'm not trying to ruin anything. . . . Uh . . . I'm just trying to—"

"A girl may look good in a fire suit, but to think you could hang with the guys is silly," Charlyn interrupted. "They're stronger, they can last longer in a hot cockpit, and they're not trying to prove anything about their gender. Plus, they don't need to check their makeup after each turn."

Jamie's stomach churned. She liked to think she was quick on her feet and could fire off a snappy comeback with the best of them. She had a lot of practice with Kellen at home. But the attack dog questions from Charlyn felt like an ambush.

She took another breath. "Just because I'm a female doesn't disqualify me from racing. I've learned a lot from watching my dad race, and I've learned a lot behind the wheel in the different levels I've gone through. The biggest lesson I've learned is that the length of your hair and fingernails doesn't disqualify you from this sport."

"But when you push your way—"

"I'm not finished," Jamie interrupted, and she could detect a smile on Charlyn's lips. "When I climb into a cockpit, the car doesn't know whether I'm male or female, and it doesn't care. Why should you or anybody else?"

"Because people's lives are at stake," Charlyn said.

"I can drive as safely as any guy on the track,

probably safer. But I don't see why people should discriminate against me just because I was born a female."

There was a long pause. "Anything else you want to say?" Charlyn said.

"Yeah. I'm not in this to make a statement. I'll climb into a race car and chase down any guy or girl or grandma. Doesn't matter to me. I want to win the cup."

TIM WENT TO THE Maxwell Motorsports garage and did what he was asked, but his heart wasn't in it. He couldn't get the DVD or the questions it raised out of his head. Who had sent that DVD? Surely Devalon knew about his part in the accident. Tim could see why Dale hadn't said anything about it, because the whole thing happened so fast and there was no way he could have seen behind him, but what about the spotters?

Tim usually got a to-do list from the bulletin board, but today was different. On Mondays, he helped unload the cars from the hauler and reload whatever cars would be used in the next race. NASCAR had taken the engine apart piece by piece in Chicago, so it didn't get here until late. Tim wondered if anybody had ever held back and taken second place because they knew they had an illegal engine. He was pretty sure it had happened.

The team had Mondays off, but some guys came in anyway. Dale clapped Tim on the back and asked what he thought about the race.

"I thought it was great when that Devalon guy hit the wall," Tim said. "I could watch the replay of that about a hundred times."

Dale laughed. "The guys wanted me to tell you what great shape the garage was in when they got here. You must have done some extra work over the weekend."

"A little," Tim said.

The sound of air wrenches filled the place, and Dale pulled Tim into the waiting room, where it was quieter. A lot of the big garages had long hallways with huge windows where tours came through to watch the mechanics work. People wearing their favorite drivers' names milled through like a museum tour, gawking at the cars. The Maxwell garage didn't have a gift shop that sold shirts and die-cast cars. In fact, the road back to the garage had only been paved a couple of years earlier when the hauler got stuck in some muddy gravel. It was definitely not in the same league with the big teams, but Dale had proved he could be a little fish and still win a race.

"We have this weekend off," Dale said. "Usually

the family takes a vacation somewhere to relax and get away. But with Jamie at the driving school, it's different. They're having a race up there this weekend that's pretty big for her."

"I understand," Tim said. "I can just hang here while you guys go."

"Well, you're free to do that if you want, but I kind of need your help."

"What do you mean?" Tim said.

"Each student is allowed a couple of outside people on her race team. Jamie has to drive a car provided by the school, but the other competitors who aren't racing join in the pits. She asked if I would be there and wondered if you wanted to join her team."

"She asked to have me there or you want me there?"

"Both," Dale said. "I suggested it and she was real glad about the idea."

Tim shrugged. "Okay."

"Good. Maybe we can head over there early Saturday and take a look around."

"If those other students are trying to win, why wouldn't they mess up somebody's pit stop?" Tim said.

"They're being watched and graded on every aspect of their performance. Plus, the pits aren't live. They get a set amount of time to be in there, and then everybody heads back out in the same positions."

"That takes the pressure off," Tim said.

"A little bit. I might spot for her or stay down in the pits. If I decide to stay, you want to spot?"

"I think I could do that."

"If you need any tips, you can talk with Scotty. He's around today." Dale turned to leave, then looked back. "You hear anything from Tyson?"

Tim shook his head. "I've called a bunch of times. Left a message with Vera two weeks ago, but she was crying. I haven't heard boo from him."

Dale nodded. "Keep trying."

Scotty was in his late 30s, about the same height as Tim, with blond hair and a blocklike body. He walked with his arms out at his sides, like he was an Old West gunfighter about to draw on a bad guy. He would have been a great cowboy, but his horse would have wanted him to lose a few pounds.

Tim had seen Scotty at races over the past couple years when he was traveling. The guy didn't talk much and seemed focused. From Dale, Tim had learned that Scotty used to race Legends and Late Model Stocks himself, but he'd been injured in a bad wreck at Hickory and had never been the same. He'd gotten married in his 20s and started a family and needed a more stable life, so he managed a golf course during the week and spotted for Dale on weekends.

"Ever been a spotter before?" Scotty asked when Tim explained what was happening.

"I've spent a lot of time thinking about what I'd say if I was up there. You guys are good, but sometimes I see things."

Scotty nodded. "Like what?"

"Like a fast car that tries and tries to get by the leader on the outside, and then he drops down and passes on the inside. If I'd have been that spotter, I would have said something about staying low in the corners."

"That's a good call. Sometimes the spotter does say something, but the driver either ignores it or has something else going on. As a spotter, you don't just concentrate on your car. You look at the whole field and anticipate."

"But how do you know when to talk and when to shut up?"

Scotty smiled. "Every driver's different. Some will want you to talk almost the whole time, telling them what you see, the latest from the officials, what you're having for dinner. Others want you to talk only when it's necessary. The thing to remember is that the driver doesn't make the team—the team makes the driver."

Amen to that, Tim thought.

Scotty talked a few more minutes, then turned to leave.

"One more question," Tim said. "Remember Talladega last year?"

Scotty crossed his arms. "Yeah, I do."

"You have any idea what happened when Dale's car lost control at the front of the pits?"

Scotty bit his lip and looked at the floor, running a toe across some imaginary line. "I was concentrating on the pit crew as he slowed. Had my binoculars on them and was talking with T.J. about the right-side tires. When I looked up, he had smashed . . . I didn't really see what happened, son. I'm real sorry about your dad."

"You must have heard stuff from the other guys," Tim said.

"Yeah, but nothing conclusive."

JAMIE WAS ONE OF 22 drivers suited up for the qualifying laps on Friday afternoon. The atmosphere was the same as a real race with a couple of the guys running off to the bathroom with a case of nerves. Jamie hadn't felt this anxious since she'd raced Bandoleros at her first Summer Shootout. She took as many deep breaths as she could without hyperventilating.

"Hope we get in the top 11," Rosa said, sitting in a plastic chair beside Jamie in the meeting room. "The person who gets the pole has the edge—don't you think?"

"True, but it doesn't mean you can't come from the back," Jamie said. "Just go as fast as you can and the position will take care of itself." The words sounded empty to her, probably because she had chided her dad when he said them and now they were coming from her own mouth.

In front of her, Chad Devalon turned. "Sounds like something your old man would say." He snickered, and Jamie wished she hadn't said anything.

Bud Watkins entered the room and the chatter stopped. Behind him walked one of the top cup contenders, and the students clapped. He had jet-black hair and dark eyebrows and a clean-cut look that Jamie saw on all his endorsements. He was known as a pretty boy, and some fans threw things at his car when he won. It seemed there was no end to their dislike. But whether you liked him or not, there was no denying he was good and that given the right car, he could win.

Bud motioned the driver to the microphone, and he stepped to the podium. "Bud thought it would be good for you to hear some remarks from somebody who knows how nervous you probably are right now. I didn't have a chance to come to a school like this, but the training you guys are getting sounds like it's awesome, so I applaud your hard work."

He nodded to Chad and a couple of others, saying it was good to see familiar faces. "I see we have a good group of females too. That's encouraging. The track is going to look a whole lot better with you guys out there."

Jamie looked at Rosa and rolled her eyes, but inside, her heart fluttered.

The driver said some other nice things and told a few stories about races he'd won and some he'd lost at the last second. "It's great to be on the pole at a race, but I've rarely started at the pole and won. Usually the best finishes I've had have come from being back a few spots. I won Denver last year from the 33rd spot, so it can be done."

Jamie remembered that race. Her dad had been leading until the late stages when he had a problem with his coolant and the engine overheated.

The driver ended with, "And I hope to be racing against a few of you in a year or so."

Somebody raised a hand. "Do you have any ritual you go through before qualifying?"

The man smiled. "I don't have any lucky underwear or anything like that. If I did, my wife would wash the luck out of it. I wear a chain around my neck with my wife's and daughter's names, but that's not for luck, just to keep me focused on what's important. I actually don't believe in luck. You prepare the best you can and use your experience behind the wheel, but when it all comes down to it, God's the one who's in control."

Jamie felt goose bumps. It sounded like something her dad would say. She'd seen this man in chapel services but didn't consider him a strong Christian. His words seemed genuine to her.

After a few more questions, the driver left.

Bud stepped to the microphone and held his clipboard up. "Here's the draw for the qualifying heats. We have 11 cars, so you'll race your laps, then come into the pits and switch out drivers. Top three qualifiers will get a bye into the finals. That leaves nine positions open. Four in each of the two heats. Got it?"

Everybody nodded or said, "Yeah."

Jamie held her pencil tight, listening for her name. It was better to be at the end of the qualifying run for several reasons. You knew what time you had to beat. The track usually was faster as well. Her name was 12th on the list. Number 22 was Chad Devalon.

Jamie set her sights on winning the pole so she could be assured of the finals and watch the competition battle for the remaining positions. Since there were only 11 cars, 11 people wouldn't make the finals.

These races were huge in their points placement for the final—where they would discover who would be given the coveted NASCAR license. Failing to qualify or to even get into the final race meant it would be almost impossible to finish on top. And everyone guessed that the top three winners of the race would probably get the prize.

Jamie walked to the track, trying to focus.

Kurt came up beside her. "Can you say _pressure_?" He smiled.

"I guess it's just part of the process," Jamie said. "To see how we'll do with it."

"You're gonna do great," Kurt said. "But what happens if one of the cars goes down or has trouble?"

"Bud said they'd rearrange the lineup and maybe drop the bottom drivers," Jamie said. "The mechanics have been working hard, but you're right—if there's a crash, that could cut the field."

"I hope I can get my rear into that #5 car seat," Kurt said. "The real cars have molded seats that fit each driver—well, of course you know that because of your dad."

"Yeah, I'll admit when I've been driving, it's been a bit roomy in there," Jamie said. "I've had to make sure the harness is as tight as I can get it or I slide around, and that's not fun in the turns."

Even though the cars had been tuned to exact specifications and everything was the same—except for the numbers on the side and the decals—everybody knew there would be one or two cars that were faster than the others. Jamie watched as the first 11 qualifiers climbed in and got set, revving their engines.

As the track warmed up, the times came down. Rosa was third in line and turned in a good time, beating the first two drivers by more than half a second. She held the pole position until the seventh driver ran faster.

Jamie took deep breaths and tried to block out the noise. She closed her eyes and tried to picture the line she'd take around the track.

Bud touched her shoulder and pulled his headphones to one side. "You want to hop in your car or you want to just visualize yourself with the fastest time?"

Jamie smirked and walked to pit road. She put both legs through the window, dipped her right shoulder, and slid in easily. How many times had she seen some wannabe at one of those driving schools do it wrong and get their shoulder stuck outside the car in some impossible position? She clicked her harness and fastened the HANS device.

Bud handed her the steering wheel, and she popped it on. He tapped her helmet and spoke into the radio. "All right, Maxwell, follow the car in front of you to the end of pit road. Stay there until you get the signal."

Another deep breath and Jamie rolled forward.

TIM'S STOMACH CLENCHED as soon as Tyson said, "Yeah?" on the other end of the phone. Tim had been calling every day and just getting a ring for so long that he was surprised to actually hear a voice.

The experience of living with Tyson and Vera flooded over him like a hurricane—the hum of the refrigerator, the smell of the trailer (like spoiled cheese), Tyson's drinking and shouting, and the bad feeling Tim had every time he heard Tyson fire up his dad's truck.

"That you, Timmy boy?" Tyson said, his voice raspy and a little slurred. It was Friday afternoon, and there was no reason for Tyson to be home. He should have been at work.

"Hey, Tyson," Tim said in a choking kind of voice.

Chapter 15

"How you doing up there? They treatin' you okay?"

"Sure," Tim said. "It's a nice place. They even found me a job working in a garage."

"Is that so? Well, that means you can pay me back for the room and board you owe me." Tyson laughed and Tim could tell he was taking a swig of something. He didn't have to guess what it was because a second later he heard the familiar clink of the beer can hitting the metal trash can in the kitchen. Tim could set his watch to that sound.

There was an awkward moment of silence before Tyson sighed. "So what can I do for you, little buddy?"

Tim's dad had called him that, and every time anyone said it, especially somebody like Tyson, his flesh crawled. "I wanted to apologize for taking something of yours. I guess you've heard by now that I got the key to that safe-deposit box of my dad's."

"Yeah, somebody called. I don't have any idea what's in there, do you?"

"No."

"You shouldn't steal people's mail. They put people in jail for stuff like that."

Tim thought that if they had a game show where people had to know all the reasons you put people in jail, Tyson would be the all-time champion. "I'm sorry I took that key. I should have just asked you for it."

"Yeah, you should have," Tyson said quickly. Then a pause. "But we all make mistakes." The top popped on another can. "Did you hear Vera left?"

"No."

"Yeah, I guess she got tired of living in the lap of luxury. I got tired of paying her bills and watching her eat everything in sight. . . ."

Tyson continued but Tim tuned him out. It was just a sad-sack story of Tyson's life, how somebody had done him wrong again. It was always somebody else's fault that he got drunk or got arrested or was late for work. In the middle of his long rant about Vera, Tim heard words he never thought he'd hear.

". . . but I don't care anymore about what your loser of a dad stashed away in some bank. You can have the stupid key. Knowing him, it's probably not worth anything anyway."

"You mean it?" Tim said.

"Have those old boys up there in Carolina call me, and I'll tell them to let you have the key."

"Wow, thanks." Tim wondered if Tyson would even remember this conversation. "I'll have them call you right now."

Tim hung up and dialed the bank, punching in the first three letters of the man's last name who had handled his case. The man's voice mail came on, and Tim left a message telling him what Tyson had said.

"So if you could call him and then call me back, I'd appreciate it." Tim left the Maxwells' number and hung up.

He let his mind run, thinking about what might be in that safe-deposit box. Maybe it was money. Maybe it was the keys to some car Tim had never seen. Or something he couldn't even imagine.

He sat and stared at the phone for a few moments, wondering how long it took somebody to get a voice mail. It was silly to think he could will the phone to ring, but he sat there anyway.

JAMIE ROLLED TO A STOP at the end of pit road and watched the official. The #11 car passed on its first lap, and she saw Kurt run high on the turn. *Don't want to do that,* she thought.

"All right, #1," the track manager said in her headset, "when you see the signal, take off."

She gave a thumbs-up outside the window net, then stretched her gloves tight and put the car in neutral. She shook her hands to get loose and stretched her feet, trying to stop shaking.

Come on. I've done this a thousand times. No big deal.

The car was hot and the smell of the racing fuel was like perfume to her. There was no breeze to speak of—the flags on the stand were limp—so she wouldn't have to worry about wind against her on the back straightaway.

Chapter 16
On Track

She pushed in the clutch, jimmied the gearshift back and forth in neutral, and finally pushed it into first. The last thing she did was flip the visor down, blocking a bit of the sun and giving her a tinted view of the track.

As the #11 car screamed past the start/finish line and slowed going into the first turn, Jamie focused on the official. He held up a hand, then pointed to the track.

"Let's see what you can do," the track manager said.

Jamie didn't pay attention to him because she was focused. The engine roared to life, and she felt that initial rush of power that threw her back in the seat. The tachometer jumped. It was all feel now, and when the engine reached its peak, she pushed the clutch in and slammed the gearshift down like lightning. Three seconds later she was in third and off the apron and up onto the track. She was in fourth gear before turn three and finding the groove low around the turn, then accelerating into the front stretch.

She caught sight of the green flag at the flag stand and mashed the accelerator to the floor. Blocking out everything, she leaned forward and tightened her grip on the steering wheel. She crossed the start/finish line and moved slightly lower, finding the quickest line into the first turn. She kept the throttle down and sped through it, creeping up a little and feeling her back end shift, getting loose, but she held it and shot out of turn two.

Good, but I can do that better next time, she thought.

The backstretch ride made her whoop for joy. The car felt solid and fast, and she could sense the speed. In turn three she kept the accelerator as far down as she could, but the rear end got loose again and she fought it into turn four.

Okay, that didn't work as well as I'd hoped. I'll make that up in the next lap.

Jamie flew past the flag stand knowing she had to make this lap a good one. Her fastest time would be used, and her first lap was less than her best. The first turn was perfect—the right speed, a good line, and no movement from behind. Unfortunately when she accelerated out of turn two, she heard an explosion that sounded like her entire car was falling apart. On instinct she gripped the steering wheel, took her foot off the accelerator and jammed it on the brake, and struggled to keep the car off the wall.

"Hold it. Hold it. Hold it," the track manager said.

A plume of white rolled over the car, and Jamie smelled acrid smoke. She came to a stop, then rolled toward the infield.

"Get out of there," the man said in her headset.

Her heart pounding, she popped the steering wheel off, released the harness and HANS device, and scooted out onto the track. She moved away from the smoke before she took off her helmet. There was debris behind the car and a huge hunk of rubber along the wall.

Two safety vehicles rolled up along with a track ambulance that looked older than she was. She waved it away.

The track manager was saying something in her headset, but she just kept walking around and around, trying to make sense of what happened.

"What was my time on the first lap?" she said to no one in particular.

"We need you to come to the ambulance, miss," the emergency medical tech said.

"No, I'm not hurt," Jamie said. "Did you see what happened?"

"Blew a tire just out of the turn," he said, his white-gloved hands taking her arm and leading her to the ambulance. "Everybody thought you were going into the wall, but you held on to it."

"The car was pulling to the right something awful," she said.

Bud jumped off another pickup and ran to her. "She okay?" he said to the tech.

"You can talk to *me*, you know," Jamie said.

Bud gave her a look.

"I'm fine. But what happens now? Do I keep my first lap time?"

"Just get in the ambulance," Bud said.

"You're not taking that first lap away from me," Jamie said.

THE PHONE RANG and Tim grabbed it on the first ring. He tried to give his deepest voice for the bank guy, but it was Jamie calling for her mom or dad.

"They aren't here, Jamie."

"I'll try their cell phones," Jamie said.

"How did qualifying go?" Tim said before she could hang up.

She sighed. "Remember what happened to Devalon in Chicago last weekend?"

"Yeah."

"Ditto for me. On the back straightaway, second lap of qualifying."

"You hit the wall?"

"No. But I left a lot of rubber out there."

"That's good. Saved the car for the competition tomorrow."

"Yeah, they're all excited I was able to save it, but my first lap wasn't as good

Chapter 17
Good Sleep

because I got loose a couple of times. I swear I could have gotten the pole on that second one."

"Where did you finish?"

"I'm in the seventh spot of the second heat," Jamie said. "I have to finish in the top four of the heat to make it in the finals."

"Piece of cake," Tim said. "You can do that in your sleep."

"There are some pretty good drivers here. I hope I can bounce back and don't get either of the two slower cars. Both the 2 and the 8 were sucking wind."

"Well, your dad said I'm on your team tomorrow," Tim said. "We'll be there to help out."

"I'm looking forward to seeing everybody." She paused, obviously distracted by something.

"I'll let you get back to whatever you gotta get back to," Tim said.

"No, hang on," Jamie said. "What about you? Anything going on?"

"Got the go-ahead from that guy in Florida to look in my dad's safe-deposit box. Now I just need to get ahold of the bank guy."

"That's great," she said, and it sounded like she really meant it. "Wonder what's in there."

"I've been wondering that for a long time." He wanted to keep the conversation going, but he couldn't think of anything else to say.

"Well, I'll see you guys tomorrow," Jamie said.

"Yeah, get some good sleep." Tim hung up and kicked himself. "Get some good sleep," he said, mimicking himself. "Don't let the bedbugs bite." *How dumb can I get?*

JAMIE REACHED HER MOM'S cell and told her and her dad the news about qualifying. They tried to encourage her, her dad ending with "Hang in there and we'll see you tomorrow." It wasn't what she was looking for. She thought she'd get some sage advice about racing, something that had happened to him when he was young, something his father had said. Maybe something she could write down on a napkin and put on her desk so she could look at it when things got tough.

Her stomach growled as she ordered her food and found an empty table. Chad sat down by her with a smirk. He had qualified second just behind a guy named Thor, but everybody called him Thunder (as if Thor wasn't unique enough). Jamie called him Lead Foot because his shoes looked like

Frankenstein's, and he always smoked his tires on the pits. Thor was another guy with a racing pedigree. His dad had driven Formula One, and his uncle had raced for the cup.

"Good job hanging on to the #1 out there," Chad said.

"Go ahead and crow about your qualifying time," Jamie said.

"Didn't hurt that you and the others warmed up the track for me. Going last helps."

Thor passed the table carrying his tray and raised a finger to say hello. She guessed he was conserving his energy for the final race on Sunday.

Jamie bit into a piece of corn on the cob, but the kernels got caught between her teeth. She worked on it as she and Chad talked, putting a hand over her mouth.

"Your dad coming up tomorrow?" Chad said. "Giving you help in the pits?"

She nodded. "What about yours?"

"He said he'd be here to watch me win on Sunday."

"Do you do that on purpose, or does it just come naturally?"

"Do what?" Chad said.

"Puff up like a big fish in a little pond, making people think you're important?" Jamie wished she hadn't said it when she saw the look on his face, so she tried to recover. "I mean, just a little humility would be so much more becoming."

Chad grabbed his tray and lifted it with one hand.

Jamie called after him as he walked away, but he was gone. Long gone.

Her cell phone buzzed, and since she suddenly didn't feel much like eating, she dumped the rest in the trash and walked back to her room talking to Cassie Strower. She had a laugh that made Jamie smile every time she heard it, even if things weren't going very well. They'd grown up together—Cassie's dad was an engineer with a popular race team in town. They were both pepperoni pizza people. They liked some of the same music (though Cassie listened only to Christian bands), and they'd spent loads of time together having sleepovers and campouts.

However, there was one thing Cassie and Jamie didn't have in common. Cassie was a thoroughly devoted follower of Jesus. She had told Jamie recently that she wanted to be a medical missionary to some foreign land where little kids were starving and needed help. Her ideas of what to do changed every few weeks, but there was no doubt Cassie wanted to follow God. She knew just about every verse in the Bible backward. Jamie joked that you couldn't see her

halo because she wouldn't stand still long enough—
she was always volunteering at the church or the food
pantry for the homeless.

Jamie had made a deal with God: *You don't bother
me and I won't bother you.* That was how she lived
mostly, though there were times when God seemed
real and almost broke through the clouds. But her
mind was usually on racing, not church stuff and
reading her Bible.

Jamie was back in her room and sitting on the
bed, flipping through the channels on TV, telling
Cassie what had happened at the track. Cassie said
she wanted to come watch the heats tomorrow, but
she was tied up Sunday afternoon.

"Don't tell me," Jamie said. "You're going to be
over at the church making meals for a bunch of
refugees."

"I didn't hear about any refugees," Cassie said,
deadpan. "Did they come from the other side of Lake
Norman?"

Jamie chuckled. "Seriously, what are you doing
Sunday afternoon?"

"Oh, it's the greatest thing ever. You know about
Camp Left Turn, right?"

"Who doesn't?" Jamie said. It was a camp put together by churches and Christian drivers that gave
sick kids a chance to go to camp for a week.

"Well, I'm going to be a camp counselor, and the orientation meeting is Sunday."

"What do you have to know?" Jamie said.

"With these kids, you have to have some medical knowledge about their disease or be able to give them support. I fit both. I've been giving myself insulin shots for years."

"Is diabetes what the kids have during your week?"

"It's why I signed up. My mom heard about a couple of people who had to back out and told me about it. I'm really excited. You should come! It would be so much fun."

"I've seen the videos of those kids going down water slides and climbing rope ladders. It does look like fun."

"I've heard their faces just light up when a real driver comes and talks to them. I can get you a form to fill out—and since your dad's a driver, I'll bet they'd let you help."

"Let me consider it," Jamie said. "I can hardly think past this weekend with the end of the school."

"With that license in your pocket, you'll be able to think a lot better," Cassie said. "You've always dreamed of this."

"It's going to be tougher than I thought. Plus, the license doesn't really let me do anything. I still have to go through the process—"

"That's my Jamie," Cassie said. "Always seeing the glass half empty. Listen, girl, do you know how many drivers would love to have that license? Some big team sees your potential, you sign a contract, get a bunch of seat time in a car, and you're off to your dreams."

Jamie smiled. It was Cassie who always saw the glass as half full. When they were little, she'd pray for dead animals on the side of the road even though they'd been there for days. The eternal optimist. "I'll think about the camp," she said, changing the subject.

"Good. I'll talk with the people Sunday and tell them about you."

Jamie talked until her cell phone ran out of battery. Then she called Cassie with the room phone, and they talked some more. It was like old times. Except Jamie had a feeling that her life was about to change. Whether it was for good or bad, she didn't know.

TIM HAD KEPT THE DVD of the Talladega accident to himself but he still couldn't get it out of his mind. Who had given it to him? And for what purpose? Was it someone on the Maxwell race team? Could it have been Dale?

Dale drove up to the racetrack, and the family got out of the Suburban.

Kellen was his usual chipper self, trying to get Tim to laugh. "I'll bet those guys have no idea what they're up against with Jamie. She can be all pretty with perfect nails and silky hair, and the next thing they'll know, they'll be staring at the decals on her bumper as she pulls away."

"That's enough, Kellen," Mrs. Maxwell said. "We don't want to give the other racers a *reason* to beat her. Like her bragging little brother."

The family checked in at the entrance

to the track, which was no Lowe's Motor Speedway, but it wasn't bad. The stands held several thousand fans, and the garage area was big compared with other tracks. They received their garage and pit passes that hung on lanyards around their necks and found Jamie. Tim had a hard time not staring at her because she was so pretty. Her hair *was* soft and silky, like Kellen had said, but her fingernails were short and her hands greasy, as if she'd been working on an engine. He couldn't believe a girl who looked like this wanted to race, but here she was in her fire suit and sunglasses, smiling at her family and hugging her mom. She punched Kellen on the shoulder when he made a comment about her muscles and called them guns. She nodded at Tim and he nodded back.

"Which heat is yours?" Dale said.

"Second," Jamie said. "And I'll be in the #7 car. There were a couple of complaints about it yesterday, but the mechanics looked it over and gave it a pass for races today."

Tim and Dale wouldn't be able to inspect it until after the first heat, so Tim and Kellen took a walk around the garage area while Dale and Mrs. Maxwell talked with Jamie.

"Should have brought a football or a Frisbee to toss," Kellen said.

Tim studied the line of cars. The school had control

of all the cars, so they didn't have to worry about people making illegal modifications, but they still watched the drivers and their crews checking out the engines. The tires were new—looked like they'd just been put on. The cars in the first heat would use two sets, if Tim gauged it correctly, and the second would use the same. The race on Sunday was a little longer.

When they came out on the other side of the garage, someone said Kellen's name. It was a dark-haired guy with expensive sunglasses. Everything about him said money. *This is the type of guy Jamie would go for,* Tim thought.

Kellen said hello and introduced Tim. "This is Chad Devalon. You should see his family's motor home. It's bigger than this whole garage."

The name cut Tim's heart like a knife. He saw the resemblance of junior to senior, though he could only see his own reflection in the sunglasses. By the way Chad kept his arms folded and didn't extend his hand to shake, Tim figured he wasn't a Christian. Every other person in the Maxwells' church insisted on shaking hands like they were about to subdue an alligator—a nice, firm grip that squeezed the blood out of him.

"I didn't know you had a big brother," Chad said.

"No, Tim's not my brother. I wish he was, but he's not. He's kind of adopted—but not really . . ."

"It's okay," Tim said to Kellen. "I'm just staying with the family for a while."

"Really? What for? You related?"

"No. My dad died, and they're letting me stay with them."

"How are you doing over there at the Maxwells'?" Chad said, lifting his head.

"Good." Tim looked around the garage. "You're not racing today?"

"Got a bye for the finals. You here to watch Jamie?"

"Actually working on her pit crew."

"I thought you were the spotter," Kellen said.

"No, your dad decided it would be better for him to do that."

"How much experience have you had in the pits?" Chad said with a smirk.

Tim was tight-lipped. "I've been around racing all my life. I know a thing or two."

Someone called Tim's name outside the garage.

Chad smiled and patted Kellen's head. "Make sure he gets those lug nuts on tight. See you kids around."

Tim sneered as Chad walked away. He couldn't stand people who thought they were better than others. Tim didn't care how many RVs the guy had or how much money or how big of a house—he wasn't better than Tim.

"Phone call for you," Mrs. Maxwell said as she ran toward them. She handed the cell phone to Tim. "It's the bank."

Tim took the phone. Weird that the guy from the bank was calling on Saturday. Maybe this one thing would go right for him.

"Tim, I received your message, and since I respect the Maxwells and we've agreed to give you another chance, I contacted Mr. Slade in Florida. I actually didn't reach him until this afternoon, and his version of the story about the safe-deposit box is different from yours."

"What do you mean?"

"I mean that Tyson told me he didn't give you permission. He denied that he even talked with you."

"What?" Tim shouted. He rolled his eyes and sighed. "Look, I talked with him yesterday, and he said it would be fine. Maybe he's been drinking, though, because his wife left. That's probably why he doesn't rem—"

"I'm sorry to interrupt you, but I can't let you lie to us and get away with it. Now if you want to go through legal channels to remedy this, that's fine, but we won't be taking any more requests from you at this office."

Tim tried to compute what the man had just said. Whatever it was, it didn't sound good. "So you're saying that even though Tyson told me—?"

"I'm saying don't call here again. Period. Unless you have some legal document that allows you to see the contents, you're not welcome here."

"Okay," Tim said. He hung up the phone.

Mrs. Maxwell pursed her lips. "Bad news?"

Tim nodded. "I guess Tyson has a shorter memory than I thought. Either that or he's just plain mean. Or maybe both."

JAMIE GAVE HER MOM a high five, punched Kellen on the shoulder (which was her only prerace ritual), nodded at Tim, then looked at Rosa ahead of her and gave her a thumbs-up.

"Enough of the niceties," her dad said in her headset. "Just get in the car and let's boogity."

"Boogie-woogie boogity." Jamie flashed a thumb to her dad high above the stands and did a quick swivel of the hips. Then she climbed in and pulled the harness tight, snapping on the steering wheel that Tim handed her. To anyone watching she probably looked loose and relaxed, but her stomach churned like she'd had a double half-pounder with cheese at the Pit Stop—what they referred to as their Heart Attack Special. She was already sweating in the 85 degree heat, and that didn't help her nerves.

Chapter 20

The first heat had been a good race, though Jamie was surprised to see how timid most drivers ran the track. It was almost as if they were trying not to lose rather than trying to win. In the end, Kurt had finished fifth, just missing Sunday's race.

"Let's not let that happen to us," Rosa had said.

Jamie fired the engine to life and followed the other cars onto the track. It was a single-file start behind a red Corvette pace car. Jamie liked the look of the car, but it wasn't anything compared to Maxie, her 1965 Mustang. Just thinking about it made her want to get behind the wheel and go for a drive. Maybe if she got a big, fat contract with some racing team she could buy a second car and fix it up.

She swiveled the wheel, sending the #7 car back and forth along the hot track, cleaning any debris from the new tires and warming them. The sun was high in the sky, and there were only a few lazy clouds rolling past.

"All right, put all the stuff you're thinking out of your head," her dad said as if he could read her mind. "Nobody out there cares how many races you've won, and nobody knows how good you are but you, so let's just show them how fast a clean driver can go."

"Are you going to do the motivational junk the whole race?" Jamie said, almost cracking up at the end.

"Looks like we're gonna do one more lap before the flag drops," he said, ignoring her.

The car felt good—not as good as the one Butch Devalon had let her drive but still fast. She let off the accelerator a little and put some distance between her and the car in front of her. She sped up into the first turn to gauge if the car was loose, and she couldn't tell. She got a surprised and mean look from the #8 driver, and she moved back into place.

The red Corvette peeled off from the line, and the cars accelerated. Jamie caught sight of a few fans in the stands. The people stood and cheered as the group came to the line. There was a rumor that a crew from a racing channel was going to be there the next day, but Jamie shut that thought out.

"Green flag. Green flag," her dad said. "Let's see that boogie-woogie boogity of yours."

Jamie smiled and shifted into fourth gear. She passed the start line behind #6 and went high in the first turn. It was there that she knew something was wrong with her wedge.

"Whoa, I'm tighter than a drum in that turn, Dad," she said. "Somebody's got the wedge way off."

She accelerated into the straightaway but had to slow before she came to the third turn. By then #8 was past her on the inside.

"We won't have a pit until halfway through unless somebody cracks up."

"Well, that somebody's gonna be me if I try to

keep up with the others and the car's this tight." She cursed. "I can't believe this."

Her dad didn't say anything, which meant he was upset and she was on her own. If she pitted before the halfway point, she would be at least a lap down. Making up that kind of distance would be nearly impossible during such a short race. But if she didn't pit, she'd fall farther behind the leader, who was already half a lap ahead.

She floored the accelerator in the straightaway and tried to make up ground, but by the fifth lap it was clear she had to come in. "Gotta pit, Dad. Get Tim ready to turn the wedge."

"He's on it," her dad said. "I've notified Bud. He says come in on your next lap."

/////

Tim grabbed the track bar wrench and stood on the wall. He knew how important it was to make the adjustment as quickly as possible so Jamie wouldn't go more than a lap down. If he did it perfectly, she could make it out before the lead car went by again. If not, she'd be in an almost impossible situation.

"Give it two full turns out," Dale said.

Tim lifted his thumb in the air as Jamie roared down pit road and slid to a perfect stop in the pit box. Tim was over the wall before she stopped, but he missed the fitting and fumbled with it—almost dropping the tool. Jamie revved her engine, and Tim felt the race leaders heading for turn three.

He hadn't worked any signals out with Jamie, but he'd seen enough races to know that when he was finished he needed to be on the inside of the car. A school official watched him like a hawk, and some of the other parents and friends crowded around the pit area to see what was happening.

Two quick turns and he threw his hands in the air. Before he even took a step to the inside, Dale yelled, "Go! Go! Go!"

Jamie shot out of the box and made it onto the track just ahead of the leader. "Oh, baby, this feels a lot better," she said as she flew out of turn four. "Tim did a good job. Got a little nervous there for a minute."

Tim put the track bar wrench away and couldn't help but smile.

JAMIE KNEW SHE'D DODGED a bullet, but making up an entire lap with the #4 car on her back bumper was a tall order. If she could put some distance between her and the rest of the field, she had a chance, but it would take the best ride of her life.

With no one in front of her, she focused on the fastest line on the track and put her foot down.

In turn one, her dad's voice came on the headset. "He's coming on the outside. At your bumper. At your door."

When her dad paused, she clicked the mic. "But not for long."

She shot out of turn two and hit the straightaway perfectly, pulling away so that #4 had to back down and follow. Out of turn four she had a two-car-length lead and the engine was humming. "Feels really good, Dad."

"All right, let's go with it. Pretend this is the start and you're in the lead. Everybody's chasing you. See if you can pull away."

And pull away she did. With the window net flapping, she hardly slowed in the turns. Six laps later, she'd made it a good :06 ahead of the nearest car.

"Caution's out!" her dad said as a plume of white smoke rose behind her.

Jamie slowed and looked across the infield to see #5 rolling toward the apron. "What happened?"

"Looks like #5 got into the wall out of turn two. A little damage on the right side, but I don't think it's serious."

"That's Rosa's car."

"Hang on. Bud's calling," her dad said.

The cars drove single file and bunched together behind the pace car.

Finally her dad came back on the radio. "Okay, pull low and let everybody pass. You're going to the back."

Jamie smiled. "Still on the lead lap, right?"

"You got it. The boogie-woogie boogity's rolling along."

She let everybody pass, and when Rosa went by she gave a thumbs-up. *I wonder if she did that on purpose to help me,* Jamie thought.

When the restart came, they were only four laps from the competition time-out. Jamie pulled ahead of two cars to put her in the seventh position at the halfway point.

/////

Tim let Kellen take the squeeze bottle of Gatorade to Jamie while he and Kurt went to work with the jack and the air wrenches. Jamie's mom rolled the new tires to the wall, and Tim put them on while she rolled the old ones away.

It wasn't the pressure of a NASCAR pit stop, but Tim wanted to make sure he did a good job and everything was fine. He moved to the left-side tires while Kellen peeled the windshield tear off and wiped the front grille. When Tim finished, he let the car down and moved to the window net. "You doing okay?"

Jamie nodded and handed him the bottle. "Good job on the wedge."

"We make a good team," he said. "Your dad's not half bad either."

"He hasn't had much to do yet."

Tim looked at the line of cars and people working. "You've got the best car out there. Show them."

Jamie smiled, and Tim thought it looked like something he wished he could take a picture of and show to his dad. *Pure joy*, he thought. *Sure is great watching somebody do what they're meant to do.*

"You forget something?" Jamie motioned to the gas tank.

"Oh, sorry. Yeah, I'll get that filled up."

/////

"Get back on track," Jamie's dad said to her. "You're in the seventh position, so we need to move up three spots before the end. Single-file restart."

The pace car pulled out when everyone was in place, and Jamie felt a lot better. She saw a number of teams working on their own wedge issues, and she hoped the adjustment they had made would be exactly what she needed to finish in the top four. Chad Devalon was behind the wall, arms folded, watching as she left the pits.

"Green flag," her dad said. "Let's see what kind of second half you've got."

She pulled even on the outside with the car in front of her in the first turn. Inches from the wall, she surged ahead and moved into sixth place when she got to the straightaway.

"Dangerous move to the top, but you survived," her dad said. "Settle down. There's plenty of time. And you don't have to win this thing. You just need to get near the front."

"I know," Jamie said. "Just showing you what I

have in me. Plus, why race if you're not in it to win, right?"

He clicked his mic and laughed.

There were moments in Jamie's life when things became clearer than others. Once in a classroom spelling bee, she had been given a word she had never heard before. From the way her stomach felt and how red her face became, it was obvious that she would never become a spelling champion. She didn't even care about being one.

Then there was the time Bobby Sizemore kissed her. A defining moment in her life because Bobby had done it on a dare from his friends, other third-grade boys, and he ran past the swing sets and into the field as soon as he'd done it. At that moment she promised herself that she was never going to let a boy kiss her again unless he really meant it.

But the big moment in her life came at Brickyard, otherwise known as the Indianapolis Motor Speedway. Any kid who had ever been exposed to racing dreamed of winning at Indy. The place hosted the biggest sporting event in the world, and even though it wasn't a NASCAR race, it captured Jamie's imagination.

Jamie's dad had taken her to the Brickyard 400 one year on a special trip—just the two of them—and he walked her to the starting line and showed her the actual bricks that were still there from the original track built in 1909. He took her to the museum to see the old cars and cases filled with trophies, along with the pictures of all those drivers kissing the bricks. At the top of the Pagoda, they looked out on a vast area her dad said could hold Vatican City, Yankee Stadium, the racetrack at Churchill Downs, the Roman Coliseum, the Rose Bowl Stadium, and the Wimbledon tennis complex at the same time.

"It's incredible," Jamie had said, trying to take in how big it was.

"Wait till all those people get here," her dad said. "More than 250,000 in the seats. Another 150,000 in the infield. The biggest football stadium holds about 100,000."

Now Jamie moved up another spot behind #2, who was in fifth place. Rosa was running fourth, and the two had made a pact to help each other, but what if they were running neck and neck for the fourth spot? Jamie hoped that wouldn't happen.

"Ten laps to go," her dad said. "It's time to make your move."

On the straightaway, Jamie passed the #2 car. She went low in turn two and shot into fifth place.

But the #2 car wasn't giving up easy. He accelerated in the straightaway and pulled beside her.

"Come on, Rosa. Move to the right," she said, wishing she had access to Rosa's headset.

Rosa remained inside and Jamie stayed behind her, actually bumping her just before they went into turn three.

"Watch outside," her dad said. "Number 2 is at your door." There was disgust in his voice. "Better move past #5. She's slowing you down."

Jamie roared down the frontstretch as the #10 car moved up behind her.

"Clear right," her dad said.

She moved right and pulled up to Rosa. Going this fast meant she couldn't take a long look, but she did catch sight of her friend for a split second. Rosa's face was tight, and she was up on the steering wheel.

Jamie kept the accelerator to the floor and only let up slightly in the turn, shooting past Rosa on the back straightaway and getting behind the #2 car.

"Fifth place," her dad said. "Two laps to go."

"Who's behind me?"

"Nobody that can overtake you if you keep your speed. You're clear high and low."

She had a choice of going low or high on #2 in turn one. She chose high, and it was almost a disaster because #2 moved high with her for the block and nearly clipped her left front.

"You're good. You're okay. Just back off and take another run at him," her dad said.

Jamie gritted her teeth and followed #2 through

the third and fourth turns. The top three cars had a good lead on them, but Jamie concentrated on #2. She saw the white flag and pulled closer, right on the #2 bumper, making them both faster.

"Take him," her dad said. "Clear high and low."

She backed off a smidge and moved slightly higher. When #2 took the bait and tried to block her, she swerved low, passing him in a blur. Number 2 tried valiantly to catch up, but Jamie crossed the finish line just ahead of him in fourth place.

"Thatagirl," her dad said. "You're going to the big dance tomorrow."

TIM FELT OUT OF PLACE in the hotel restaurant where everyone went that evening. When he and his dad ate out, it had usually been at places where you could get a burger or a taco in a few seconds. This place was a lot nicer, and with all the dirt Tim had on him, he went to the bathroom and scrubbed his hands.

While he was in there, the #2 driver came in, banging the door against the wall and stalking like Godzilla. Behind him were Chad Devalon and the guy Jamie called Lead Foot. The bathroom had two sections, and the three went on the other side of the wall to talk.

"It was a dirty move and you know it," the #2 driver said.

"Yeah, Kenny, it was dirty, but you weren't racing her. You were blocking her," Chad said.

"You should have just kept that line

at the bottom," Lead Foot said. "I don't think she could have caught you."

"Too late now," Kenny said. "I'm out. And you guys are in."

"We'll get her back for you," Chad said.

The urinal flushed and Tim didn't hear what they said next. He tossed his paper towel in the trash and headed for the door.

Chad noticed him. "Well, if it isn't the Maxwell grease monkey. You get all the grime out from under those fingernails? Wouldn't want the girls in there to get grossed out by your bad hygiene."

Tim pushed past them.

But Kenny put his hand on the door and blocked him. "Tell that girl of yours she'd better watch her back tomorrow. We don't like dirty drivers."

Tim was going to walk away, but something sparked inside him and he turned. "She beat you fair and square. You know she's a better driver than you. Better than all three of you."

Lead Foot laughed. "Looks like Grease Monkey has a girlfriend."

Chad shook his head and scrunched his face. "You *do* like her, don't you? Must be hard living that close to somebody and knowing she'll never see you as anything but an oil jockey."

Kenny scoffed. "He's lucky that family took him

in. I can see it from Maxwell's point of view. He gets somebody to change his oil and mow his yard for just three meals a day and a place to sleep."

Chad took off his sunglasses. It was the first time Tim had actually seen the guy's eyes. "You know Jamie goes for guys like me."

"She hates your guts," Tim said.

Lead Foot laughed. "Yeah, that's why she eats dinner with him just about every day."

"Jamie has a thing for me. That's no secret. And she wishes she could drive as well as I can."

"She's going down tomorrow," Kenny said. "Better have a box of Kleenex over there in the pits for after the race. She's gonna need them."

Tim grabbed the door handle and stared at them.

The guys stepped away, and Chad put his sunglasses back on. "Enjoy your meal."

JAMIE DIDN'T HAVE a chance to talk with Rosa at the track, and she looked forward to seeing her at dinner. A few of the drivers shook her dad's hand and said hello. They all said, "Good job out there" to Jamie and she smiled, but until she got on the track and proved herself in the final race, the words felt empty.

Tim came to the table but didn't look at Jamie. Everybody was acting squirrelly at a time when they should have been celebrating.

Kurt sat a few booths away, and Jamie went over and asked if he'd seen Rosa. He shook his head. "Saw her go to the elevator, but she didn't look in the mood to talk."

"Sorry you didn't make it into the finals," Jamie said.

"Maybe if we'd have been in the same race we'd have both made it," he said. "Congrats. You're gonna have your hands full tomorrow."

Jamie picked at her food as Kellen talked about a movie he'd seen, quoting the funny stuff the characters had said and laughing so hard he snorted. Jamie only half listened. She was thinking about her strategy from the back of the pack. That and Rosa. She excused herself from the table and hurried to Rosa's room and knocked on the door. The TV was up loud— a music channel.

The sound clicked off. "What?" Rosa said.

"Housekeeping," Jamie said. It was their inside joke. Anytime somebody said something in a class or butted into a conversation they'd look at each other and mouth "housekeeping," for the staff at the hotel that always seemed to come to make the bed at the worst time.

Rosa didn't laugh. "Go away."

"Rosa, come on. I need to talk."

"You need to go away." Her voice was choked, and it reminded Jamie of her own voice after she'd had a fight with her parents.

Finally Rosa opened the door enough for Jamie to see her red eyes.

"Look. I'm really sorry about the race. I—"

"You have no idea what this means," Rosa interrupted. "Do you know what it took to get me to this place? I *had* to get into the finals for there to be any chance of me ever making it in racing."

"That's not true," Jamie said. "You can bounce back from this. Just chalk it up to experience and—"

"There's stuff you don't know," Rosa sobbed. "My mom works at a hotel like this. In housekeeping. I've worn hand-me-down clothes all my life, and I've driven cars other people didn't want, and I've tried so hard."

"I'm really sorry. I tried to help you out there, and I would have pushed you across the finish line if I could have. . . ."

The elevator door opened, and another driver got off.

Also on the elevator was Bud Watkins. He held the door. "You two coming down?"

When Rosa heard Bud's voice, she closed the door, disengaged the lock, and stormed out, still in her fire suit. "This was unfair and you know it," she said, tears starting, her jaw set. "You said there'd be a level playing field, but it's not anywhere near level."

"There's probably a better place to talk about this," Bud said, taking his hand off the elevator door.

Rosa put her hand there. "No. This is good. Letting that Chad guy in on our racing school, especially after other people had been let go, is not fair."

"You should have said something earlier."

"I couldn't say anything because you'd have pinned my ears back. If that Chad guy hadn't been here, I would have made it into the finals."

"Maybe," Bud said. "But that's the way things go in racing. It's a good lesson to learn. There's a lot of things that aren't fair. Like what's happened to . . ." Bud looked at Jamie.

"What?" Jamie said.

"Nothing. I'll announce it at our—"

"No, Mr. Watkins. What are you talking about?"

Bud sighed and looked at the elevator floor, then the buttons, then the ceiling. Everywhere but at Jamie and Rosa. Finally he cleared his throat. "There's a problem with one of the cars. No way we can fix it by tomorrow."

"What kind of problem?" Jamie said.

"That's not important. The point is, we're down to 10 cars. You had the lowest qualifying time of any of those in the finals. That means you're out."

IT LOOKED LIKE SOMEONE had hit Jamie in the center of the gut with a telephone pole and then whacked her again as she walked back to their table. Her mom and dad asked what was wrong, and she told them. Tim thought it took a lot of guts not to cry about it—girl or guy, that kind of news was devastating. To work as hard as she had obviously worked and not get into the finals had to hurt.

"What's wrong with the car?" Tim said.

"Yeah," Kellen said. "Tim can fix it."

Jamie shook her head. "On the last lap, one of the cars blew a piston right out the side of the engine block. Bud said it looks like somebody took a shotgun to the thing. It's that bad."

Dale nodded. "That'll take some time."

"What about the car Devalon said you could use?" Kellen said. "You know, the orange one."

A spark came into Jamie's eyes. "We could get it over here tomorrow morning, couldn't we, Dad?"

"If they'll let you," Dale said. "We can bring it over tonight."

Jamie ran off to the front of the room to talk with the main guy, who looked like he enjoyed telling her no. She came back, shoulders slumped, and it was clear what had happened.

"Why can't you use it?" Kellen said.

"It's not an approved car here. He said it wouldn't be fair." She put quotation marks around the "wouldn't be fair" part with her fingers.

"I'll tell you what's not fair—letting Chad in at the 11th hour," Mrs. Maxwell said.

Tim watched Dale. The man's mind was going, trying to figure a way around the situation. Tim had seen this happen before with drivers and crew chiefs. They were given a problem and then had to figure out an answer. But Tim could also tell the guy was holding back a lot of input. Maybe he wanted this to be Jamie's fight and was struggling with not getting too involved. Tim respected that because any other parent would have been jumping down the organizer's throat.

The main guy, who had a name badge on that said *Bud Watkins*, walked over to the table and shook hands with Dale. "I'm really sorry about all this, but I don't think there's anything we can do."

"We appreciate you considering all the options," Dale said. "She's worked really hard to get into the finals."

Jamie just gritted her teeth. Kellen nibbled at some cold chicken fingers. Mrs. Maxwell had a napkin in her hand balled up tighter than a baseball.

"Can't we postpone the race?" Jamie said.

Bud shook his head. "We're opening up the stands for the finals. Plus, one of the racing channels said they're sending a crew to do limited coverage. They'll be here tonight to set up."

"Maybe it'll rain," Kellen said.

Tim wiped his mouth with a napkin as Bud turned to leave. "Excuse me, sir?" Tim said. He couldn't believe that was actually his voice coming out of his mouth.

Bud turned and squinted at him.

"This is Tim Carhardt," Dale said. "He's staying with our family now."

"Carhardt?" Bud said. "Are you Martin's boy?"

"Yes, sir," Tim said.

"I'm real sorry about what happened," Bud said. "What can I do for you?"

"Uh, I was looking around in the garage and saw another car under a tarp. Another #4 car."

Bud looked at Dale and snickered. "Snoopy little buzzard, isn't he? What about it?"

"Well, it looks like the same size engine. The body's dinged up and the paint's peeling, but if it'll run, why couldn't Jamie race that one?"

"The body damage isn't the problem," Bud said. "The truck arm bar snapped. That goes from the axle—"

"I know where it goes," Tim interrupted. "We can fix that, and I'd bet Jamie doesn't care what the thing looks like." He stole a glance at Jamie, and there was fire in her eyes.

Bud rubbed his stubbly beard and looked around the dining room.

"I'm willing to work on it all night if we have to," Tim added.

"Me too," Kellen said.

"Where would you get the parts?" Bud said.

"We've got parts in our garage," Dale said.

Bud took in some air through his clenched teeth and glanced at Dale. Tim noticed a smile come over Dale's face as he lifted his eyebrows as if to say, *Why not?*

"Stay here. I'll be right back," Bud said.

"I've never seen that other car down there," Jamie said when Bud was gone.

Tim shrugged.

"If I get in that race tomorrow, it'll be because of your idea."

Though he tried not to, Tim blushed. He walked over to the ice cream machine to make a sundae and stayed there, lingering over the sprinkles and the nuts and the caramel sauce, then the chocolate.

Bud returned a few minutes later after talking with someone at the front of the dining room and then calling someone on a cell phone. When he walked over to the Maxwell table, Tim watched. At first, he couldn't read anything from their faces. Then Jamie let out a squeal and jumped in the air and actually *hugged* the old Watkins guy.

Tim just laughed.

JAMIE AWOKE THE NEXT morning and at first couldn't figure out where she was. It wasn't until she saw the poster of Dale Earnhardt over her desk that she realized she was in her own room. She hopped out of bed and looked at the garage. Her dad's truck was gone.

She grabbed her robe and hurried downstairs and found her mother at the kitchen table with her Bible open and a cup of coffee in her hand. She was using her favorite mug—the one Jamie had made in art class with her mom's name on the front and a cross. "Did Dad leave for the track? Or church?"

Her mom smiled. "He hasn't gotten home yet. Tim and Kellen are with him."

"They've been working all night?"

"They thought they had it all ready,

but Tim found something wrong with the air filter, which led them to the carburetor. They had to put in a new one."

"Wow" was all Jamie could say.

"I talked with him a half hour ago. He said not to expect too much with the color, and there may be some power issues, but at least you'll have a ride."

Jamie shook her head. "I feel bad for staying here and sleeping."

"Don't. They wanted you to be fresh."

Jamie made some toast to settle her stomach. It was doing flips and turns, and she thought some of her mom's freshly canned blackberry jam would do the trick. It didn't, of course, but it tasted so good she didn't care.

"I feel bad about church," Jamie said. "This is one of the few chances Dad has to go to a regular service during the season."

"Honey, he wouldn't miss this for the world," she said. "Reminds me of all those go-kart races we used to go to. He couldn't wait to see the look on your face when you got out there on the track."

Jamie sat with her mom, listening to her turn the onionskin pages and looking out at the pond just down from the garage. A few ducks and geese walked around the edges, then flew to the middle. It was a lot prettier here than at the hotel. Somehow she felt like something had changed between her and her parents. She'd begun the process of leaving—she knew that—but it felt weird, like she was a stranger in her own house. And Tim . . .

"What's going through that head of yours?"

A mist came over Jamie's eyes, and she didn't look at her mom. (That was the last thing she wanted to do.) "I don't know. I was just thinking about Tim and how he must miss his dad and what it would be like to lose somebody so important."

"I heard him crying in his room the other night and wanted so badly to go in and talk, but I didn't."

"Do you know anything about his mother?"

Her mom pursed her lips. "Just that she hasn't been in his life for a long time. I don't think anybody knows where she is."

Jamie was quiet for a minute. "I know I gave you a lot of grief over having him come here. But, for the record, I think it was a pretty cool decision."

Her mom smiled. "Thanks for saying that. I hoped you'd feel that way."

"Kellen probably wants him to be permanent. Sure likes him better than he does me."

"Kellen couldn't be prouder of his big sister. He's your number one fan."

Jamie nodded and the mist got thicker. "What do you think about college? I mean, after I get out of high school. If I have a chance to race, should I go for that or do the college thing?"

"You have plenty of time to make that decision. But I don't see why you couldn't do both."

Jamie stood as the truck pulled into the driveway. She went out to meet her dad.

Kellen couldn't stop talking about all they'd done to the engine to make it ready. "You should have seen Tim. He found stuff even Dad's full-time mechanic didn't see."

"Your mechanic was there?" Jamie said.

"He left around four this morning," her dad said, giving her a hug, then taking her by the shoulders and keeping her about an arm's length away. "Now, we don't promise you the best-looking car on the track or even the fastest. But it will be safe and you should be able to finish. Where you finish is up to you."

"Thanks, Dad. I'm going to do my best to make your work worth it."

They all went inside, and Tim and Kellen headed for their bedrooms.

Her dad kissed her mom on the forehead and said, "You want to try and make the nine o'clock service?"

Her mom closed her Bible and smiled. "I'll get ready."

TIM WAS STILL YAWNING just before race time, but that meant he was relaxed. At least, that's what he told himself. The stands were about three-quarters full, which was pretty amazing. He'd seen one of the tickets that said *Tomorrow's Stars Racing Today*, and he'd wondered if any of these drivers would actually make it. They all had a chance, of course, but he'd seen so many younger drivers come up and then go down.

Before the national anthem, a pastor prayed for the safety of the racers and everyone involved. Tim thought of his dad and how that prayer hadn't been answered at Talladega. He tried to put that out of his mind and focus. Both Rosa and Kurt, Jamie's friends from the school, helped in their pit box. While the other racers walked past him without noticing, these two at least said hello.

Chapter 26

Kellen was a ball of energy, and it was all his mother could do to keep him from jumping in the car himself. Tim just laughed at the kid. He was going to make a great driver or baseball player or something someday.

Chad Devalon walked past with his sunglasses shining and eyed the car. He ran a hand along the painted *1* they had put in front of the *4* that had been there.

"Nice touch," Chad said to Tim. "Like father, like daughter."

"Maybe like Chicago," Tim said. "I think Dale finished first there, didn't he?"

Chad sneered at him, as if talking to him were a capital offense. "Wouldn't have if people hadn't raced dirty."

"I thought your dad blew a tire," Tim said. "Maybe the tires are racing dirty."

Jamie walked up, her helmet and HANS device already on. "Better head up there to your car, Chad. But don't get used to being ahead of me."

Chad gave her a wispy smile, like one of those guys in the movies just before he gives the girl a big kiss. "Just make sure you wave when I lap you the first time. And the second. And the third." He gave the car a pat and shook his head. "This thing will be lucky to stay on the lead lap." He walked to his car and climbed in.

Tim had the headset on, so he heard Dale say to Jamie, "Whatever Devalon said, put it out of your mind. Show him what you can do on the track."

"Yeah, I got that," Jamie said as she got in the car and strapped in.

Tim handed her the wheel, and she slammed it on like she was really ticked off. She gave him a thumbs-up. He leaned down to say something. He'd been practicing all night as he worked on the engine and found the problem with the airflow that would have slowed her down. Dale had patted him on the back for that and said, "Good catch."

"You're better than all these guys," Tim said. "Show 'em what you can do."

Jamie flipped up her visor. "What?"

He patted the top of the car twice. "Go get 'em."

He unhooked the generator from the oil tank just as someone's voice came over the loudspeakers. "Gentlemen and lady, start your engines!"

Nine cars fired to life. Jamie's car didn't even sputter. Jamie tried it again but nothing happened.

"Switch over to the backup box," Dale said over the headset.

Jamie flipped the switch and tried again, and the car fired to life. It was the best sound Tim had heard in his life.

Jamie followed the rest of the pack down pit road

and onto the track behind the pace car. The only thing that made the #14 car stand out was its lack of a slick paint job. All the other cars looked like the best NASCAR had to offer. Hers looked like some spotted pony in the Kentucky Derby.

The camera crews were out, recording the race for playback later—probably at midnight on some Wednesday if Tim was right. Still, they were here, and with the fans cheering, it had the feel of a real race.

Mrs. Maxwell came up and put an arm on Tim's shoulder as Jamie crossed the start/finish line, zig-zagging to clean her tires. Tim worried the engine wouldn't hold up for the whole race, but so far it looked and sounded good. Jamie gave a thumbs-up out the window net and pulled closer to the car in front of her. It would be a single-file start.

Never thought I'd be rooting for a girl to make it into NASCAR, Tim thought.

GREEN FLAG. Go! Go! Go!" Jamie's dad said to her.

She punched the throttle and flew high and past the #9 car at the line. No problem with the engine here at the start. It had plenty of zest. Clearly #9 was surprised at being passed, because he tried to push her high in turn one, but she blew past him.

"Got a long way to go," her dad said. "Take it easy and get your legs in this new car."

"Feels good, Dad. You and Tim did a great job."

"Let's wait to see what happens when this is over."

Jamie settled in and rode in the middle of the second pack—a dangerous place to be if there was a crash. In the past two days the biggest wreck had been on pit road, where two cars had gotten into each other. A few had grazed the wall, but that was it.

Jamie caught sight of the leaders a quarter of a lap away. Chad was ahead and seemed to be pulling away.

Don't worry about catching him, Jamie told herself. *Just get past this pack.*

"Best line is at the bottom of the track, Jamie," her dad said. "That'll be the easiest."

"Looks like everybody else thinks you're right," Jamie said. "There're three ahead of me low."

On the 10th lap, Jamie saw smoke ahead of her.

"Go high. Go high. Go high," her dad said.

Jamie swerved high and barely missed a tangle of cars.

"Good job avoiding that mess. Yellow flag."

"What happened?"

"Number 6 got a little wobbly in turn three and got into the #7. Then #7 went down to the barrier and did a Darlington below the grass. Looks like he's out."

Ever since Jamie was a kid, she and her father had used code words from his former races. One year at Darlington he had been bumped by one of the most popular drivers when he was riding the inside line. In turn four, the two of them collided, pushing her dad to the infield, slamming into the barrier and sending him to the hospital. The other driver recovered and went on to finish fifth. Anytime somebody got bumped and was sent down, they called it a Darlington.

Jamie pulled in behind the #5 car and followed the pace car as the debris was cleaned off the track. As she passed the #7 car, Roger, one of Chad's friends, climbed out. He looked okay, but she could tell he was frustrated.

She tried not to glance into the stands during a race, but when they were driving under caution, she'd sneak a peek at the grandstands and look for signs. She picked out a crude one that said, "#14 is #1! Go Jamie!"

The next time she came around, she caught sight of Trace Flattery, a guy in her youth group and a school friend. She could see him because he was one of the largest people in the stands, and judging from his red face, he was yelling the loudest.

I swear, if I had a horn on this thing, I'd honk at you, Trace, she thought.

"Going to green the next lap," her dad said.

Jamie had a good restart, passing another car for fifth place. At the halfway point she was solid there when she went in for new tires and a full tank of gas.

"You've gone from #10 to #5 in the first half," Kellen said, giving her some Gatorade in a squeeze bottle. "Next half you'll get to first."

"That's what I'm gunning for," Jamie said.

"How does it feel?" Rosa said when she had finished fueling the car.

"It's handling like a dream," Jamie said. "Just a little wobble in a couple of the turns, but it feels even better than the car yesterday."

Rosa nodded. "You're half a race from a license. Show them we can do it."

Rosa slapped Jamie's hand, and Jamie knew she meant that she needed to show the guys that the girls could actually race. "I'll do my best."

Chad Devalon led the first half with a two-car lead over the #4 car, driven by Dante Irving, the only African-American still racing. Thor was in third place in the #1 car. Jamie started the second half in fifth place and rolled out of pit road gritting her teeth.

"You ready for this?" her dad said.

"I can't wait," Jamie said.

THE NEW TIRES felt great, and Jamie picked up speed as they headed for the green flag.

Her dad clicked the microphone. "Lotta guys talking about you up here."

"They like my hair?"

"They like your line and the fact that you moved a reject car up to fifth. Guys calling the race are watching you real close."

"They're probably the ones who like my hair." She laughed. "Tell them I'll have my nails done in the network's colors if I win."

"We got a green flag. Go. Go. Go."

Jamie shot forward and pulled even with the fourth-place car. By the time they reached the start/finish line again, she was in fourth and closing on third place. She checked her gauges as she went low, in sight of Chad and the other two in front of her.

Chapter 28

In her head, Jamie could hear one of her favorite songs playing over and over. She liked to listen to a group whose lead singer was a Christian and wrote all the music. Even regular radio shows, not just Christian stations, played their music. Bobbing her head, tapping on the steering wheel, she was in her zone. The cockpit was her favorite place in the world because here she felt in control, at home, and it was a place where she could use the skills she'd learned through years of driving. The dirt tracks came back to her—the go-karts, the Bandoleros, and even the dirt bikes she had raced a few times (before she realized she preferred a steering wheel to handlebars). The soundtrack of her life played in her mind as she again sped around turn four.

Before she knew it, she had pulled even with Dante, who had fallen back to third, on the outside, but the guy wasn't giving up his position without a fight. They drove two wide with Jamie leading into turn one and Dante zooming ahead out of turn two. Chad was just ahead, with Thor a car length in front of him.

For some reason, Chad slowed on the inside, blocking Dante, who drove up behind him and nearly bumped him.

Jamie sped into turn three, and when she hit the throttle out of turn four, she was right beside Devalon.

"Careful here, Jamie," her dad said. When he used her first name, she knew he was concerned. "You never know what this guy is gonna do."

She glanced over at Chad for a second and caught a flash of sunlight on his visor. She roared into the first turn going high.

"Number 4 is right on your tail," her dad said. "Use his draft and take this puppy in the straightaway."

Chad shot out of turn two, but Dante's draft helped her gain speed, actually pulling her ahead as she hit the third turn.

"Clear left," her dad said. "Take him."

She kept the throttle wide open and moved left, all the time thinking that her mom would kill her if she made that kind of move on the interstate without giving a signal.

"Second place now. Let's finish this field off and bring it home."

Jamie wanted to scream and pump her fist, but they were a long way from the end. Thor was two car lengths in front and holding low, coming close to lapping a few other drivers.

"Look ahead of you," her dad said. "You're about to lap #9 on the inside. If you can get to the outside of #1, you'll have him trapped."

"Hammer down," Jamie said, shooting forward and going high into turn one. They caught up with the

#9 car on the straightaway, but Thor swerved around him at the last second, cutting Jamie off and nearly sending her into the wall.

"Jerk," Jamie said. "I'm going to enjoy beating this guy, Dad."

"Calm down and keep your head. You don't *have* to win this thing, you know."

Jamie frowned. "You think I'm out here to come in second? That's not how you race."

Her dad laughed. "You got a point. I'm just saying a top-three finish will be okay."

With 10 laps to go and Chad and Dante breathing down her exhaust pipe, Jamie saw her chance when Thor swung high into turn one.

"Clear low," her dad said.

She cut to the bottom and sped out of turn two. With clean air in front of her and the rest of the field watching, she took the lead and stretched it.

"All right, you got the lead. Now let's see what you can do with it," her dad said.

Jamie felt like flying right out of the cockpit when she saw the others lagging behind. She rode the line of her dreams and took the car past the start/finish line, glancing at her pit crew and seeing Kellen standing on the wall, pumping his fists in the air. It made her go faster.

"Four laps to go," her dad said. "You're doing great."

She choked back thoughts of what the ceremony would be like when they finished. She hadn't planned a speech. Would the guys with the cameras be there to interview her?

With those questions in her mind, she noticed smoke behind her near the wall and cursed.

"Yellow flag," her dad said.

"What happened?" she yelled.

"Devalon. He nudged the #9 car into the wall as he lapped him."

"You know he did that on purpose, Dad. That's not right."

"Just slow down—and hang on. Okay, they're calling you into the pits. We're into overdrive."

TIM FELT THE EXCITEMENT in the pit area as drivers pulled in and waited for the debris cleanup. Chad Devalon's car had sustained some damage on the right side, and there were a couple of guys pounding on his front quarter panel.

Kellen moved close to Tim. "That's Butch Devalon talking to Chad. Meanest racer there is."

"I know about him," Tim said.

Jamie took a drink of Gatorade and Tim leaned down. "We just gave you enough fuel for the last laps."

"Did you see what Chad did?" Jamie said. "You know he turned that guy so they could catch up to me."

Tim nodded. "I doubt they'll call him on it, though. Guys like that can get away with a lot of stuff the rest never do."

Jamie fumed inside the cockpit. Tim

wanted to say something to encourage her, but he couldn't think of much. Finally he repeated something he'd heard over the radio before. "You've run a real good race. Let's bring it on home."

They waited for the signal to reenter the track. It would be a green-white-checkered finish. Green flag to restart, white flag signaling one lap to go, then the checkered flag. If there was an accident on any of the laps after the green flag dropped, the field was frozen and would finish in that order.

Tim looked at Devalon again. His professional pit crew worked on the car making a small track-bar adjustment. Butch gave a signal, and they added a splash of fuel.

Dale came on the radio and tried to calm Jamie. "You're out first. Head to the end of pit road and follow the pace car."

Mrs. Maxwell and the others cheered her from behind the wall, but Tim could tell Jamie was in a zone. Just as she pulled onto pit road, Chad cut her off. She had to brake and her engine stalled. Butch Devalon laughed.

Jamie fired up the car again, and something in the engine's restart bothered Tim. As she revved it a couple of times, he heard something weird. He knew what it was, but he hoped he was wrong.

JAMIE FOLLOWED the pace car out of the pits in first place. Thor followed in second, Dante was third, and Chad fourth. Four others were still on the track, but everyone knew these four had the fastest cars. Would someone try to outmaneuver them?

She passed the area where Chad had crashed the #9 car and saw the skid marks. She shook her head and tried to stay focused, moving left to right to keep the tires warm and remove any debris. The last thing she wanted was a blown tire.

They went an entire lap around before the restart, and Jamie's stomach knotted. She knew there was a split second where she could win or lose the race—and that was near the start/finish line. It was a single-file restart, and when the pace car veered off, she kept her speed and slowly moved toward the line.

"Nice and easy," her dad said. "You know what to do."

The green flag waved, and Jamie punched the throttle and surged ahead, the engine screaming as she zipped past the line. She could tell by glancing at her side mirror that she'd hit the restart just right. Out of turn two, she had a two-car-length lead.

"Devalon's making his move," her dad said. "Don't worry about him, though. You got this thing. You hear me? And here comes the white flag. Bring it home."

Her heart raced. She couldn't stop smiling. She concentrated on staying low in the turns and riding the momentum out of it. She couldn't wait to see the look on Chad's face when she stood in the winner's circle. He was closing in on her, but if she drove this last half of a lap smart, she had first locked.

On the back straightaway, with the checkered flag being pulled in the flag stand, Jamie felt the engine miss. Her stomach fell as the engine coughed and sputtered even though she held the accelerator to the floor. Chad gained on her as she lost speed.

"I've got a problem," she said.

"You've got smoke out of the rear," her dad said.

"Something's not right." Jamie kept her foot all the way to the floor as she hit turn three.

Chad ran high and pulled beside her, then shot ahead in an incredible burst of speed as they came out of turn four.

"It's slowing up!"

"Push it to the finish, Jamie!"

Thor pulled beside her and passed. Then Dante was next to her. With the finish line in sight, white smoke filled the cockpit, but she didn't let go of the steering wheel or ease up on the throttle.

"The field should be frozen right now," her dad said, but no one was listening.

Dante pulled away as her engine finally gave up with a final pop and more smoke poured out. She put it in neutral and coasted across the finish line in fourth place.

"Get out of there," her dad said. "Get out. Get out."

She popped the steering wheel and loosened her belts. As she unsnapped the HANS device, someone ran to the car through the smoke. Tim took off the window netting and helped her out as she coughed and sputtered worse than the engine.

She tore off her helmet and stared at the car. Fans screamed, and Chad smoked his tires and tore through the infield like he'd just won the Daytona 500. Jamie looked away and saw her mom and Kellen still at the wall near pit road. The medical crew arrived and checked her out, but she pushed them away.

"I heard the thing giving way when you restarted the engine heading out of the pits," Tim said. "I knew what was going to happen. It was only a matter of when."

"Why didn't you tell me?"

"Wouldn't have made any difference. You had to push it to the end. Just let it happen."

"You okay?" her dad said on the headset.

"Yeah. Why didn't they freeze the race?"

Her dad didn't answer.

The crowd cheered Chad. Thor stood on his window opening and raised both fists.

Dante was the only one who walked away from his car and asked how Jamie was. He gave her a pat on the back. "Tough luck. You were the best on the track. You know that, don't you?"

The words brought the first tears to her eyes, and she looked away, wiping at them. "Yeah."

When Butch Devalon walked over, Jamie couldn't stand it. She headed toward the garage to avoid him.

But he cut her off. "Now just hold on. You ran a good race out there."

She pointed a finger and narrowed her eyes. "Your son cheated. He doesn't deserve that license, and you know it."

"It's just a racing thing. You've got to learn that, little girl."

It was all Jamie could do not to run at the guy and give him a head butt.

Tim stepped between them and pushed her toward the garage. She could tell he was just as angry and that felt good. He didn't say anything to Devalon, but she thought she heard him muttering something as they walked away.

"Don't be upset," Devalon called after them. "We can still work something out with our team."

Jamie shook her head as she took the clip from her hair and let it fall.

"You walk away now, Jamie, and it's over. You understand? You come back here."

Jamie kept walking.

EARLY THE NEXT MORNING Jamie walked to the lake, sat on the bank, and watched the fog lift from the water. The day after big races she'd come here to sit and think and try not to let a win or a loss affect her. The frogs croaking, the crickets chirping, and the water gently lapping against the shore gave her a feeling she couldn't explain. Something about it could cool the elation of winning or take away the disappointment.

Except today. Nothing could take away the empty ache inside. She'd come as close to winning as a person could. She'd been one spot away from getting a real NASCAR license. Now she'd lost that and probably her chance to race for Devalon—though she couldn't even think about being on that guy's team after what had happened. This morning they were awarding the licenses, and she couldn't bear to be there.

Jamie tossed a few rocks at the water, then pulled grass and threw it. She didn't hear the footsteps behind her and was surprised when her father sat down, stretching his legs so that his big boots nearly reached the water. He had a mug of steaming coffee in his favorite cup, a black #3 on the outside.

"I heard you leave this morning," he said. "Figured you'd be out here."

She sighed. "You really need to get rid of those jeans. Even the holes have holes."

"Hey, they're just getting broken in. Besides, if I don't have some little quirky thing like this, your mother won't have anything to complain about. I'd be perfect, right?"

"That's not what she says," Jamie said, smiling, though there was a growing feeling of sadness deep inside.

They sat there a few minutes without talking.

Finally her dad broke the silence. "The paper had a little write-up about the race. Whoever wrote it knows you were something special out there."

"I guess that's what they call a consolation prize." She sighed. "It's not fair. And I know racing isn't fair, that there are bad breaks and you have to take the good with the bad and all that, but I worked so hard. . . ." Jamie put her head in her hands and felt his strong hand on her shoulder.

"I know. And I'm sure proud of you for finishing school, going through all that training and pushing yourself to the limit. I can tell by the way you drove that you learned a lot."

"But what good does it do?" she said. "Devalon's not going to let me race for him. I sold my car and put everything on that school to get noticed."

"Believe me, any team would be proud to have somebody like you driving for them. It won't be long until you're out there pushing those guys like nobody's business."

Jamie shook her head, her heart breaking.

"Look. I know you have to find your own way. But even if the Devalon thing worked out, I don't think you'd have liked it over there. Let me finish the teaching you need. I can help you get where you want to go."

"Dad, we just don't click."

"We clicked out there yesterday. And when you spotted for me at Daytona, we had some good chemistry—don't you think?"

Jamie picked a few more blades of grass and tossed them in the water.

"You have the skills to be one of the best. You have the drive and the competitive edge a lot of people just don't have. When you were two, you couldn't stand losing to me at Candy Land. Remember that?"

"You always got Queen Frostine," she said.

"But you also have compassion," he continued. "You are exactly the type of person this sport is looking for. You're a good role model. You race clean, yet you can be aggressive. A little too aggressive at times, but you'll learn. I couldn't be more proud of how you acted after that race yesterday. You could have gotten into it with Devalon and those goons, but you walked away."

"Tim pushed me away. If it hadn't been for him, I probably would have taken the track bar to Devalon."

Her dad smiled. "I want to help you. Let's get a plan together and make it happen. With Indy coming up this weekend and a win under my belt, who knows? I might even make the Chase."

"Can that happen? I mean, statistically it can, but—"

"Don't count the old man out yet," he said. "I still have some fight. I'd love for you to be there this weekend."

"I'm supposed to go to this camp for little sick kids tomorrow with Cassie," Jamie said. "It lasts all week."

"I'm supposed to be their featured driver this

week," he said. "I'll get you a flight on Saturday or even Sunday morning if you'll come."

"Okay."

A fish surfaced and ate a bug on the water. The sun rose behind them through the trees, red and angry. The light from it made the clouds turn purple and orange. Looking at the scene, Jamie said, "I thought God was going to let me win that race. I thought that's what he wanted for my life. I can't tell you how much it hurt."

Her dad just sat there and stared at the water. Then he crossed his legs and scooted closer. "Life is a process of becoming who you are and not who you're not. Does that make sense?"

"Seems kind of obvious."

"Well, it's not, really. A lot of people never learn it. With each choice you make, you choose who you are and who you aren't. And each experience shapes who you're becoming."

Jamie threw some more grass.

"My dad quit school in the 10th grade to go work on cars with his dad. He made a choice about who he was going to be. Now, I wouldn't agree with that choice today—I wouldn't want anyone to quit school for any reason—but that's what he did. In my life, I choose every day who I'm going to be with all those drivers out there. They want me to have some beers with them or go to bad places. I want to be liked by those guys like kids in high school want to be liked by their peers. But I have to make a choice. Who am I going to be?"

"They make fun of you. They call you a goody-goody or a teetotaler."

"I know," her dad said. "And how I react to that is a choice I'm making of who I'm going to be too. I used to want to fit in so badly that I'd go drinking with those guys just so they wouldn't tease me. Then I realized I was letting them decide who I was going to be."

"What happened?"

"They still make fun of me. But let something happen in their lives—something bad like their wife leaves them or a child gets sick or any of a hundred things—and who do you think is the first person they come to?"

"You?"

He nodded. "I can't tell you how many times it's happened. They want to know what somebody like me thinks because their friends are out chasing some kind of happiness they'll never find. They see me as a guy who's stable and doesn't have to have all that stuff to make him happy."

Jamie and her dad had rarely talked like this. She'd seen how he lived his life, but she'd never heard his reasoning. It always seemed like he was just a guy who didn't want to have fun. Now it sounded like he was the one who had found what he was looking for and didn't have to chase something that would slip through his fingers.

"God throws stuff at you every day," he continued. "Either that or he allows things to happen. Choices to make—little things like what to look at or not look at, what to think about or not think about. So many people think that being a Christian is walking an aisle or saying a prayer or being baptized. It's true that you have to respond to God's invitation. You have to accept the gift he's offering. Once you do that, the deal is sealed. God doesn't give you something and then take it back. Can you imagine a parent giving their kid a gift on Christmas, then because they spilled their milk, taking it away from them?"

"I remember when you threatened to take that Barbie away from me if I didn't take out the trash."

Her dad smiled from ear to ear. "That's not what I'm talking about."

"Bad choice you made, huh?"

"My point is that becoming a Christian is a once-in-a-lifetime deal. You ask God to forgive you and tell him you're sorry for all the bad stuff you've done, and if you really mean it down deep and you're not playing games, God takes you seriously and he comes in. Becoming a Christian is his deal. He's the one who works in your heart to draw you to himself. But here's the tricky part. *Being* a Christian is different. The Christian life is made up of all the choices you make from that day on. You can choose to ignore God if you want. You can choose your own way. But if that decision was real back there when you asked him to come in and take control, you won't do that for long. You'll want God back on the throne where he deserves to be."

"So choosing God and letting him take over doesn't mean I'm going to win."

"Nope. Besides, if you won every time, it wouldn't be special. Losing makes the winning even better."

"So he's testing me, in a sense. With this loss, I mean."

"Doesn't just happen on the track. I'll bet there were some kids who disobeyed the rules back at the school. Tried to sneak out and go to a party when they knew they'd get in trouble."

"I was invited to a couple of those parties."

"There you go. And how did you decide?"

"I didn't go. I told them I didn't want to lose my spot—"

"No, not *what* did you decide. *How* did you decide?"

Jamie thought about the question. "I guess I just

weighed whether going out with them was worth getting kicked out of school."

Her dad nodded. "That's a mature thought. Did it ever enter your mind what God thought about it?"

"Honest?" Jamie said.

"Yeah, shoot straight."

Jamie took a breath. "I'm not even sure if I believe like you. I mean, I know Jesus died for me and that he was God and all the stuff I've learned in Sunday school since I was little." She could feel some emotion in her voice and a tremble in her chin. "But I don't think I can be like you and Mom. And Cassie. She's like a little angel that prays every second and always thinks about other people."

"I'll admit, Cassie is a little hard to live up to. But you don't have to compare yourself with her. Don't you see? That's the same kind of peer pressure only in reverse."

"I don't get it."

"God wants to come into your life and forgive you and make you a new person. But the person he wants to make you is not Cassie. He wants to make you the best *Jamie* you can be. The *Jamie* he created you to be."

"But won't I have to go off and become some missionary to people who've never seen a NASCAR race?"

"You mean like New York City?" her dad said, laughing.

She chuckled, but then the dam broke and she started to cry. Her dad hugged her tight, and she didn't want him to let go. When she was 12 or 13, he stopped hugging her for some reason, and then he went to some conference and when he came back, he hugged her every day and she got sick of it. Now it felt good just to be in his arms and let go of her emotions.

"Jamie, I know God is doing something in your heart. I can tell it. Your mom can tell it. I think he's preparing you for something really big. And the choices you make each day help bring you closer to who you really are. Who he really wants you to become."

"But I don't even know if I'm really a Christian."

"Do you want to follow Jesus with all your heart?" he said softly. "Do you want to choose him and not your own way?"

"Yeah."

Her dad let go and leaned down a little to look her in the eye. "Do you want him to strap into the driver's seat and drive? Jamie, you've been driving the car of your life a long time. Climb out and let him take over."

Jamie nodded, and through her tears she said, "That's what I want."

At the edge of the lake, with the water rippling

from a fishing boat that passed a few hundred yards away, they prayed together. Though Jamie still felt the sting of the loss the day before, her heart soared. And she couldn't wait to talk with Cassie.

Someone yelled for her, and the two of them stood. Kellen came running across the field, holding up his mom's cell phone. He tossed it to her, out of breath.

"Who is it?"

"Some guy . . . Watkins, I think . . . from the driving school . . ."

JAMIE MET CASSIE in the parking lot of Camp Left Turn the next morning. Cassie was excited and hugged her. "You said you had news for me?"

Jamie nodded. "The guy who ran the driving school called yesterday and said he wanted to meet me today. I told him I'd be here."

"What's it about?"

"Maybe an honorable mention or something," Jamie said. "I'm not holding my breath."

"Well, I think you handled it really well. My dad was in the stands, and he said he hadn't seen anything so heartbreaking since the Earnhardt blown tire at Daytona."

"He put that tire up on the wall in the garage to remind him how close they came."

"You should do the same thing with

that engine," Cassie said, then shook her head. "It's still probably pretty raw for you, isn't it?"

"Yeah, but I think I have a better perspective on it now. Because of what happened yesterday."

"What do you mean?"

Jamie told Cassie about her talk with her dad and what she'd decided about her life. "I want to do whatever God wants me to do. If that means racing, I'm all in. If it means following you to some foreign country to carry your Bibles, I'll do that too. Except I want to drive."

Tears filled Cassie's eyes. "You don't know how long I've prayed for this. Not that I think you're some heathen or anything. I could just tell how much you were struggling through school and in church. It seemed like you really wanted to know God, but something was holding you back."

"I think you're right. I was scared that I had to be just like you."

Cassie squinted. "Me? Why would you be scared of that?"

Jamie folded her arms. "You know. You're so . . . faithful and holy and—"

Cassie held up a hand. "Hang on. You have no idea. I let God down all the time."

"Right, like you had an extra scoop of ice cream when you were six."

"No, I've done some bad things."

"Name one."

"Well, being jealous of you."

"Me?"

"You've got all the driving talent in the world. You can take an engine apart and put it back together faster than my dad. And you're the dream date of every boy at Velocity High."

Jamie rolled her eyes and chuckled. "I guess we always want to be something we're not—when what we are is just fine."

Cassie hugged her again. "Oh, I almost forgot. I want you to meet someone. Come on."

As Jamie followed, Cassie explained about the campers and how they handled their diabetes. "Most of the kids here can give themselves their own shots, but some of the young ones need help and monitoring."

"Must be hard having to take shots every day. I wouldn't want to take even one."

Jamie followed Cassie to the dining area shaped like a race car. In fact, just about every building in the place was shaped like a race car. A blonde girl with blue eyes was eating, swinging her legs under the table. She had a cute smile and a #14 hat on.

"This is Jenna," Cassie said, sitting down across from her. "And, Jenna, this is the girl I was telling you about. Jamie—"

"You're Jamie Maxwell?" Jenna said.

Jamie smiled. "I'll bet you know my dad."

Jenna's mouth dropped open, and her fork fell onto her corn dog and green beans. She was drinking a diet soda. "I can't believe I'm actually meeting the daughter of Dale Maxwell. I saw your dad in person at Daytona. I mean, I almost saw him. And you were spotting for him, weren't you?"

Jamie couldn't believe the girl knew so much. "Yeah. But why didn't you get to see him race?"

"I'd saved up my money and everything, but that's when I got sick. I have diabetes." Jenna pronounced it *die-beetees*. "They had to take me from the track straight to a hospital, and they stuck needles in me to give me fluids and stuff. Now I have to take more shots."

Jamie looked around and noticed Cassie had left them alone. "Does it hurt?" she said.

"Sometimes," Jenna said, some mustard covering her top lip. "But if I don't have my insulin, I feel really bad, so a little stick is a lot better than feeling bad all over."

"Sounds like you know your stuff. What's that black bag?"

"Oh, that's to take my blood sugar. I have to stick one of my fingers and see what the level is to make sure it's not too high or too low."

"How old are you?"

"I'll be nine in June," she said.

"You mean, next year?"

"Yeah, but I like to say it that way because it makes me feel older, you know?"

Jamie laughed. "What's the best thing about this place?"

Jenna looked up at the ceiling like she was trying to figure out some math problem or the correct air-flow for a Lexus. "Well, I like the pool and the slide a lot, and the climbing wall was fun. Oh, and the counselors are really great. Cassie's my favorite, but maybe you'll be my favorite after today. But . . . probably the best thing is that I don't feel so all alone."

"What do you mean?"

"Well, at my school, I have to go down to the office and get a shot just before lunch. My mom comes and gives it to me. I feel kind of weird there because I'm the only one in my class who has die-beetees."

Jamie nodded. "I've felt kind of alone like that before too."

"But here," Jenna continued, "everybody is just like everybody else. We all have die-beetees, so nobody gets taken to the office for a special shot. We all go."

Jamie smiled. The two talked for a while, and then she pulled out her cell phone and dialed. "Dad? There's somebody here who wants to talk with you."

TIM RODE ALONG with the Maxwells to Camp Left Turn.

Mrs. Maxwell said she was looking forward to coming here. "Dale's been before and I came last year. Just the look on the kids' faces when they see Dale or some of the other drivers is worth the trip."

"I'm not sure I want to be around a bunch of sick kids," Tim said. "What if it rubs off?"

Kellen laughed. "You can't catch diabetes from somebody like a cold."

"Yeah, but some weeks the kids are really sick, right?" Tim said.

"None of the illnesses are contagious," Mrs. Maxwell said. "You don't have anything to worry about."

As they made the hard left turn into the parking lot, Tim asked Dale what he was going to do.

Chapter 33

"I usually just walk around and talk to the kids and watch them ride horses and swim. Then they get all the kids together in the main building, and I answer questions."

"What are you going to say?"

Dale unlocked the doors. "That your life isn't defined by your problems. You might have difficulties, and you may have caught some bad breaks, but you don't have to let those hold you back. The kids who come here could let whatever illness they have stop them. They could become the little sick kid. But the truth is, they don't have to be known as that. They don't have to give up."

"Most of the best home run hitters struck out a lot more than they homered," Kellen said. "And if you race NASCAR, there are 42 losers and only one winner in each race."

Tim watched as Dale was mobbed as soon as he walked through the gate. The kids ran to Dale like he had some kind of kid magnet and wouldn't stop following. Some wanted autographs, some had questions, and some of them were too scared to do anything but stare. It wasn't until Dale sat on a bench and got eye level with them that the timid ones approached.

"Do you think you have a chance for the Chase, Mr. Maxwell?" one boy said.

"I'm running well right now, but there are a bunch of drivers ahead of me. It's hard to catch up because they're all scoring points too. I'll know more after this weekend in Indy."

"Are there any drivers who are diabetic?" a boy said. "My mom said I couldn't be a long-haul trucker or serve in the military, but what about NASCAR?"

"If there's not a driver now, why don't you become the first one?" Dale said.

The kid smiled so wide and shook Dale's hand so hard that Tim couldn't help smiling too.

Then Jamie walked up with a little girl. "Dad, this is Jenna. She came to Daytona to watch her very first race, and that was the day she got sick."

"I'm sorry to hear about that, darlin'," Dale said. "Have you been able to come to another race?"

"Dad had to save up a long time for us to even come to that one," Jenna said. "And I saved my allowance. Maybe next year."

"I'll tell you what," Dale said. "If I get in the Chase, you and your parents ought to come down to Talladega to see that race. I could get you some tickets if you want."

"Are you kidding?" Jenna said, her eyes wide. "Just one thing. You'd better make it, because I really want to go."

Everybody laughed and Tim did too, but there was

something about hearing the word *Talladega* that sent a shiver through him. How would he feel going back there? Would the Maxwells even invite him?

They moved to the track area, where Dale was introduced by a man with a microphone. The crowd cheered, and the guy even introduced Jamie as "an up-and-coming driver you're sure to see out there one day."

Jamie blushed and waved at the kids, then settled in with her friend Cassie.

Dale told some stories about his favorite races and his least favorite wrecks. He showed the kids a couple of his techniques of driving and finished with a Bible story about Noah and how God told him to build a holy race car.

The kids laughed and said, "No, it was an ark!"

"Well, it was a special vehicle, and when Noah finished building it, do you know who got in and drove?"

The kids were silent.

Dale said that God shut the door himself, and it began to rain. Then he said some things about letting God have control of your life, and he glanced over at Jamie and winked. Most of the stuff Tim didn't pay attention to because he was looking at the parking lot. The Watkins guy from the driving school walked up to the back of the audience and just stood there, staring at him.

JAMIE SHOOK HANDS with Mr. Watkins, and the man nodded, his face grim. He said hello to her mom and shook hands with her dad. The kids were still gathering around, and Bud asked if they could go to someplace more private.

Jenna pulled on Jamie's dad's hand. "My mom told me if I really got to see you, I should give you this." She handed him an envelope.

He put it in his shirt pocket and knelt before Jenna. "I hope I'm going to see you a little later in the season."

She smiled and walked away with the rest of the campers.

Jamie followed Bud toward the parking lot. When they were outside the fence, Bud leaned against his truck and pushed his hat back a little, crossing his arms *and* legs. He just stood there for a moment, and Jamie wanted to scream for him to say something. She turned and saw Cassie over by the meeting hall watching them.

"We've got a situation with the race Sunday," Bud finally said as Tim and the others walked up. Bud stared at Tim for some reason.

"What kind of situation?" Jamie said.

"We're DQing one of the teams."

"They're going to send one of the drivers to Dairy Queen?" Kellen muttered.

Jamie punched her brother's arm. "One of the top three?" she said.

Bud nodded. "The Devalon team. Since he won the race, we gave the engine a good once-over and noticed some residue. It looks like they put some additive in his fuel. Jet fuel to give him an edge."

"Why would they do that?" Jamie said. "He didn't need it."

"Well, evidently they thought he did." He looked at Tim again. "Or, if we believe the crew, somebody put the stuff in their fuel can."

Tim looked away.

"What are you going to do, Bud?" Jamie's dad said.

"Unless they can prove that someone sabotaged their fuel, we're pulling his license and giving it to the one who finished fourth."

Jamie's mouth dropped open, and she tried to resist the urge to jump up and down and scream.

Bud stepped toward Tim. "You have anything to say about this?"

"It's a real shame, sir. I don't like cheaters any more than you do."

"Did you have anything to do with it?"

Tim shoved his hands into his pockets. "Why would I want to help them win the race? I'm on the Maxwell team."

"You could have known we'd find that residue and would have to DQ him."

"That seems like a stretch," her dad said. "The simplest explanation is that they gave Chad a splash of that stuff to power him to the finish. Or that he was running with it the whole race."

"They said they saw Tim in their pit area," Bud said.

Her dad looked at Tim square in the eyes. "You have anything to do with this?"

"Absolutely not," Tim said, not hesitating.

"That settles it for me," her dad said. "We don't have that kind of fuel additive around our shop anyway. Where would Tim get it?"

"We're going to review the video from the race, but as it stands right now . . ." Bud faced Jamie. "Little lady, you just won yourself a license."

When Bud reached out a hand to shake, she couldn't help hugging him.

"We also looked over your engine," Bud said. "What you did with that car from start to finish is nothing short of amazing. I hope you know that."

"We had a good run," Jamie said, glancing over at Cassie. The girl's head was bowed and her eyes closed. Jamie wished she'd stop praying so she could give her a thumbs-up.

"If I were you," Bud said to her dad, "I'd get that girl an agent. She's the best I've ever seen at her age."

Her dad smiled. "She's the best I've seen. Period."

AT FIRST, TIM COULDN'T believe the Devalon people would accuse him. Then he figured he was a likely candidate in their minds. They probably thought nobody would stand up for him. People would just throw him under the bus like they always did. They hadn't planned on Dale and Jamie.

The next day, Butch Devalon showed up at the house while Tim was outside weeding the flower garden for Mrs. Maxwell, his shirt off. He had some music on a headset as he pulled and picked. When that black truck parked in the driveway, he shut off the music and wiped the sweat from his brow.

Devalon walked over to him. "Why'd you do it? Why'd you want to ruin Chad's chances?"

Tim didn't want to back down. He wanted to stand up to the guy. But he remembered something his dad had said: *"When you wrestle with a pig, the only thing that happens is you both get dirty."* The DVD came back to him, and he gritted his teeth. It was like staring down some fire-breathing dragon.

"I don't think your son had any right to be there, mister. From what I hear, he came in halfway through and didn't pay his dues like the others. But I didn't do anything to his stupid car. You've got nobody to blame but yourself."

The man snarled at him—Tim could swear the guy snarled like a dog—as the door opened behind Tim. He kept his eyes locked on Devalon as the man looked up.

"What can we do for you, Butch?" Dale said.

"Tell your daughter to get out here."

From the creak of the porch, Tim figured Dale stepped down a step or two. "I'd advise you to change your tone a bit."

"I don't need any advice from a loser like you. Now tell her to get out—"

Jamie's car pulled into the driveway, and she stopped just past Devalon's truck. Tim found his shirt and put it on. Mrs. Maxwell came out on the step and rested a hand on her husband's shoulder. Kellen came over from the barn. It was like they were all there to watch some bad reality TV show.

Jamie got out of her car in a sweat-stained T-shirt and her workout shorts. She went to the gym at least once a day. She walked up to the group, looking at Devalon, then her parents.

"The deal's off," Devalon said. "I don't want your kind on any team of mine. And I want the key to my garage back. Now."

Jamie nodded and ran inside. She returned with the key and tossed it to the man, who caught it with one hand.

"Don't ever come to me whining about wanting a second chance," he said.

"I never asked for a chance in the first place," Jamie said. "The truth is, my dad's going to teach me everything I need to know from here on. And he's twice the driver you'll ever be."

Devalon shook his head and laughed. "Him?" He looked around at the house, the barn, and the garage in the distance. "Yeah, this place is a monument to the success of Dale Maxwell. He's built quite a racing empire."

Mrs. Maxwell walked down the steps and stood on the concrete sidewalk that was a little cracked. She put her hands on her hips. "Being a driver isn't just about winning, Butch. It's about being a real man to your wife and family."

"Nicole, don't get all upset because you picked the

wrong guy to marry. It's okay to be jealous of what I have. Might even be an incentive for your man to work harder."

"You got what you came for, Butch," Dale said. "Now leave."

"Yeah, leave," Kellen said, his voice strained.

"What goes around comes around," Devalon said, glaring at Tim. Then he looked at Dale. "Watch your back at Brickyard. You never know when something bad'll happen."

"Good-bye, Butch," Dale said.

Devalon shoved the key in his pocket and walked back to his truck.

Tim started his music again and watched the black truck zoom down the driveway, sending a cloud of white dust over the yard and into the trees in the distance.

JAMIE SAT IN ON the meetings with her dad and the crew as they chose a car for Indianapolis. T.J., the crew chief, wanted to use a backup they'd tuned especially for Indy.

But her dad wasn't convinced. "I won the race in Chicago with that engine. I'm really comfortable with the car and the way it ran."

"No modifications?" T.J. said.

"Why mess with a winner?" Dale said.

Jamie had driven a backup car on the track with him, going through his practice routine. The main thing she needed at this point was seat time. Scotty had heard about an opening at a driving course and mentioned it to Jamie. She called, but because she was only 17, they wouldn't consider her. The fact that she had a license and was

Chapter 36
The Verse

Dale Maxwell's daughter interested them, but they wouldn't waive their rule.

Jamie drove to Indianapolis with her mom, Kellen, and Tim. They couldn't get a second room at the hotel, but Scotty said it was okay if Tim stayed in his room. When Kellen begged to stay too, saying he'd sleep in the bathtub in his sleeping bag if he had to, and Scotty agreed, Mrs. Maxwell relented.

It was a gorgeous day in Indianapolis. Hot and muggy, but the sun was out and the track looked great with all the colors and the fans. Her dad came into the race 16th place in points. Not bad considering his performance in the past few years, but to jump to 12th place and make it into the Chase in five races would be difficult—if not impossible—especially with the talent ahead of him.

The sponsor problems her dad had experienced (his main sponsor had threatened to pull out in the spring) had lessened once he had won in Chicago. There were several stories in magazines and on Web sites about the "comeback" of Dale Maxwell. Each one had mentioned Jamie's finish at the driving school. Others noted that a popular beer advertiser had offered to bail the team out, but Maxwell had said he'd quit racing before using a beer sponsor. There had been a lot of controversy—including some drivers upset that someone like Jamie could get a license when she was barely 17 (her birthday had come in early June) when NASCAR required drivers to be 18. Because the school had been started by NASCAR, they waived the rule but gave each venue the choice to let her drive. Since Jamie had no team and she was only listed as a backup for her dad, no one thought there'd be a problem.

At the chapel session before the race, the chaplain talked about leaving a legacy to your kids. At first, Jamie didn't think it was for her because she couldn't imagine getting married, let alone having children. But the more the guy talked, the more she saw her dad's influence in her life. She decided that a legacy didn't have to start when she was older and had a family—it could begin right where she was. When the guy prayed, she closed her eyes and asked God to help her give a legacy to her family that began early.

The family went from there to the pit area and greeted other drivers. Jamie's mom had a tradition of giving a printed verse to other drivers she knew were believers.

Jamie thought she had handed out all of them when Butch Devalon walked past them in his black outfit and black shoes.

"Hold up there, Butch," Jamie's mom said. "I have something for you."

He glanced at the piece of paper she handed him.

Then he looked at her. "This supposed to be some kind of Christian curse on me?" he growled.

Her mom smiled. "Not a curse. A blessing. I wanted you to have that to show there were no hard feelings. And that God is real and wants you to turn to him."

He shook his head and threw the piece of paper on the ground. "I needed help from him a long time ago, and it never came. Keep your religious mumbo jumbo to yourself."

When he had gone, Jamie picked up the paper from the asphalt. It read, *Psalm 46:1—God is our refuge and strength, always ready to help in times of trouble.* "Why'd you give him that one?"

Her mom shrugged. "It was supposed to be for another driver, but he didn't qualify. Just kind of stuck out to me."

"What did he mean about needing help from God a long time ago?" Jamie said.

Her mom thought a moment. "There are things about people we'll never know. I met Butch when he was about your age. Had a rough life. Real rough. Maybe one day he'll see his need for God."

Kellen walked by with his "Legend in the Making" T-shirt on. "I'm not holding my breath."

"Stranger things have happened, young man."

"Yeah," Jamie said. "Like Kellen taking a bath."

Kellen just laughed.

Her dad came over and hugged them. "No family fights during the race now." He kissed her mom, and she whispered something to him and handed him a piece of paper. He read it and then wiped away big tears. "See you at the winner's circle," he said.

Jamie asked her mom what she had said.

Her mother smiled. "There are some things I say to only one person in the world. But I will show you the verse I gave him." She pulled out her pocket New Testament and opened it to Hebrews.

Jamie read, "'Therefore, since we are surrounded by such a huge crowd of witnesses to the life of faith, let us strip off every weight that slows us down, especially the sin that so easily trips us up. And let us run with endurance the race God has set before us.'"

"It's not *exactly* about Indianapolis," her mother said, "but it still fits, I think. Let everything else go and concentrate on the race ahead."

TIM STOOD BEHIND the war wagon, watching the crew chief talk to Dale during a yellow flag. A few weeks ago Dale had been the one caught in a wreck or running over debris. Now he was racing like he belonged up front. He had his extra points for leading a lap and could pick up even more since he had been in front 45 of the 160-lap race. Currently he was running fifth and gaining quickly on the leaders.

"You're about three seconds behind the front," the spotter said. "Separated from the rest of the field. Maintain that position high and you'll move up in the straightaway."

"Number 7's backing off a lot," Dale said.

"He's losing downforce because of a lift in the front. Getting a lot more air down there than the other cars."

Tim switched to the race coverage and heard the announcers talking about Maxwell. "That win in Chicago really energized old Dale," one commentator said. "He looks like he's a man on a mission right now, and I wouldn't want to be in front of him."

"And there's one driver who Maxwell won't have to catch. Let's go down to the pits and hear from Butch Devalon. Butch, this is the second race in a row where you've failed to finish because of an accident. What happened out there?"

Tim turned and looked at the camera just outside the infield care center, where Butch Devalon stood. He was wearing a headset with a microphone on it.

"I don't know. This is just how it goes—long season and lots of chances to hit bumps in the road," Devalon said. "We'll be back at 'em next week."

Tim walked over and stood a few feet behind the cameraman, staring at Devalon. When he started talking about being confident he would finish at the top of the Chase, Tim shook his head and acted like he was laughing, doubling over and holding his stomach. It didn't faze Devalon, but it felt good to try to distract him.

What didn't feel good was getting a peck on the shoulder and turning around and seeing Chad Devalon. "What's wrong with you, punk?" Chad said.

Tim shrugged and walked away.

"You're the reason I got DQed!" Chad said.

"You're crazy," Tim said. "I never touched your car."

Chad clutched Tim's shirt and pulled him back. The guy's face was red, and his neck veins stood out.

"Leave him alone!" someone yelled behind him. It was Kellen, who had grabbed Tim and tried to pull him away from Chad. In the midst of the commotion, Tim heard the announcer say something about "a commotion in the pit area." He turned to see the camera trained on him and Chad and Kellen.

"I think that's Butch's son down there," the commentator said. "He doesn't look too happy."

A guy with a badge and two big arms took the three away to a security area inside the care center.

Chad fussed and fumed until his dad came for him. He looked even madder than Chad.

"Enjoy the rest of the race," Tim said as they walked out.

"Good one," Kellen said.

A TV showed the lap count—only 25 to go, and Dale had moved up to third. Kellen could hardly sit still beside Tim, but when his mom came into the room with the guard, he shrank into the seat.

"Sorry, Mrs. Maxwell," Tim said. "Chad Devalon kind of jumped me, and there was nothing I could do."

Mrs. Maxwell talked with the security guard and he released them. "What was it about?" she said.

"I guess he's still sore about losing that race," Tim said. "He thinks I did something to his car."

The crowd stood on the south stands and gasped.

Tim put on his headset and listened. "It wasn't Dale. It was a group in the middle of the pack."

"Yellow flag's out," Kellen said. "That'll eat up a few more laps for Dad."

When the white flag came out, it was just Dale and another driver racing for the win. Dale tried to catch him in the last turn but came in second by less than half a second.

"And that second place finish catapults Dale Maxwell all the way to number 15 for the Chase."

"That sounds like a long way out of number 12," the commentator said, "but with four more races to go, I wouldn't bet against him."

Dale made his way to the group afterward and hugged his wife. Jamie compared notes and told him what she would have done on that final turn. Dale laughed and put an arm around her. Then a cloud came over his face when Butch Devalon walked up behind them.

"Keep that Carhardt kid away from me and my family, Maxwell," Devalon said. "You hear me?"

"I heard you, Butch. You okay?"

"Don't pretend you care about me or anybody but yourself. Just keep that menace out of the pits. I've filed a formal complaint against him. He'll never get in here again."

OVER THE NEXT FEW WEEKS, Tim spent lots of time in the Maxwell garage, watching and learning everything he could. He never dreamed he'd be this close to seeing the inner workings of a crew. When he traveled with his dad, he'd watched stuff happen from afar. Now he was right in the thick of it.

Though Tim had never been a math whiz, he tried to calculate Dale's chances of making the top 12. It all depended on what the leaders did, of course, but if he finished in the top 10 in the next four races and the driver in the #12 spot faltered at all, Tim figured he still had a chance.

Butch Devalon's filing had sealed Tim's fate at races. He wasn't allowed at any more during the year unless the officials changed their minds. He could tell Dale was disappointed with him, especially after he'd seen the video coverage. When Tim explained, Dale nodded but said, "You could have avoided all that by not trying to distract Devalon."

"Yes, sir," Tim had said.

The Wednesday evening before Michigan, the day before school started again, Kellen came to get Tim in his room. "Phone call for you. Some guy who sounds like he wears a suit to bed."

It was the man from the bank. "Mr. Carhardt, have you received the box yet?"

"What box?"

"Oh, I'm sorry. We sent the contents of the safe-deposit box to Mr. Slade in Florida two weeks ago, at his request. He said he would send the items on to you. He told me he mailed them last week. You should be getting them any day."

"Did he say what was in there?" Tim said.

"No, I'm sorry. I'm hoping this clears up any problems for you."

The guy was being awfully nice to him, especially for somebody who told him never to call his bank again. "Okay. Thanks."

The next day was the first day of the new school year. Tim rode with Jamie in her Mustang, and the engine sounded like a dream. Mrs. Maxwell had bought Tim several new outfits to wear to school, supplies like notebooks and pencils, and a new backpack that Tim couldn't wait to try out.

"What's it feel like to be a senior?" Tim said.

"It hasn't really hit me yet that I'll be done after this year," Jamie said over the song on the radio.

"You going to college?"

"My parents want me to. I'd rather just race."

"Maybe you can do both. Kellen said you were going to Denver with your dad."

"Yeah, I've never been to Colorado. That new track out there is supposed to be something."

"Drink a lot of water," Tim said.

The day dragged by, and Tim wondered how he'd ever get through it. He rode the bus home because Jamie finished earlier than him. He stopped at the mailbox at the end of the driveway and found several clothes catalogs and junk mail, but there was one colorful postcardlike piece that had his name on it. He ran all the way to the house and showed Mrs. Maxwell.

"Do you know what this means?" Tim said.

"It must be the box from Tyson," she said. "Looks like we owe some money on the package."

"I'll pay for it," Tim said.

"Nonsense. How was your first day back?"

"Okay, I guess." Tim fidgeted like a kid who had to go to the bathroom while Mrs. Maxwell called the post office.

She came back with a frown. "The carrier still has it with her, and she hasn't made it back to the post office yet. They said I could pick it up tomorrow morning. I can do that and bring it by the school."

"That's okay," Tim said. "I've waited this long. I can wait one more day."

TIM DIDN'T SLEEP much that night, and when he did, he dreamed that Tyson was hovering over him, waiting to pounce on him for opening his mail.

The next morning as Jamie drove him to school, she said, "What do you think's in that box?"

Tim shrugged. "Something I guess my dad wanted to protect. I still don't know why he let Tyson have control over it, but he did."

"He probably just wanted to make sure there was someone who could take care of you," Jamie said.

Tim scooted down in his seat. "He couldn't have picked a worse person."

Jamie seemed a lot older than Tim, even though she was only 17. He wanted to say something to make her laugh, to make her like him, but he felt like a pimple on the nose of life. There was a dance at the school tomorrow night and he thought about asking her, even though he couldn't imagine getting up the courage to do it.

Finally he blurted out, "You heard about the dance Saturday?"

"Yeah," Jamie said. "I usually don't go because of the racing, but you might have a good time. Mostly people just stand around and drink punch and listen to music. I'll be in Colorado."

"You just going to watch or to work?" Tim said.

"Our PR rep has a wedding she wants to attend. She's dating Billy Reuters, the driver of the #72 car."

"I know who he is. Little guy who'd bump his own grandmother out of the way."

Jamie laughed and Tim felt like a million bucks.

"That's pretty good. I think he'd probably spin his own grandmother out on the last lap of Daytona if he thought he could win."

"So, you're going to rep for your dad? That's good. Maybe when she gets married, you'll have a place on the team."

"No offense, but that's not my dream job. I want to be behind the wheel, not writing PR copy."

"Yeah, I guess that'd be a step down for you."

Tim had noticed a change in Jamie. She didn't act as on edge and she seemed happier. At peace with herself. At first he thought it was getting the license, but it seemed deeper than that. Something had happened to change her perspective.

Jamie's mouth dropped open, and she turned down the radio. "Hey, you know who would go with you? To the dance, I mean?"

"I didn't say I wanted to go."

"I know, but if you were thinking about it, I know someone who would go with you. Just as a friend."

His mind wound through the few people the two of them actually knew. "Who?" As soon as he asked, he thought of Cassie Strower. Of course. Jamie and Cassie were best friends. But Cassie was so spiritual she'd probably kiss him if he promised to become a Christian, then want to baptize him as soon as their lips separated.

"Cassie," Jamie said. "She really likes being around you. She says you're a breath of fresh air at the youth group, not like the rest of the people who just say stuff because they want the leader to like them or other people to think they're spiritual. You should ask her."

"I don't think I'm in her league. Plus, I'm not a Christian, and she probably wouldn't go to a dance with anybody who hasn't memorized the whole Bible backward."

Jamie laughed again, and Tim thought making Jamie laugh would be a good job. "I'm surprised she'd even go to a dance."

"She doesn't go unless there's a reason," Jamie said. "You know, she's on some committee to set up the room or something. And I used to think the same thing about her—that she had some halo around her head and wouldn't be interested in anything but praying and eating locusts like John the Baptist."

It was Tim's turn to laugh, but it was more of a chuckle and he automatically threw his hand up in front of his mouth so Jamie wouldn't see the space between his front teeth.

"You have a great laugh," Jamie said. "You ought to do it more often."

Tim looked out the window and saw the school in the distance.

"I could talk to Cassie if you want and get back to you?" Jamie said as a question.

"No, but thanks," Tim said.

Tim was in Spanish when a principal's aide called for him to come to the office. He took his books because it was near the end of class and said adios to the teacher. She smiled and returned the farewell.

Mrs. Maxwell was waiting for him with a package under her arm. She had a way of smiling that made Tim feel like he actually mattered. Since his dad had died there were very few people he'd actually let inside his world, and he'd had a few late-night talks with her that he couldn't imagine having with anyone else on the planet. He'd had a counselor in Florida, but he always felt weird paying for someone to listen to his troubles. It probably worked for other people, but he couldn't get over the thought that he just wanted to say what the counselor wanted to hear so he could get out of there.

Mrs. Maxwell was different. He didn't have to be anything but himself around her. He even let a few bad words slip, and he thought she'd want to wash his mouth out with soap or make him write "I shall not cuss" a billion times. But she hardly flinched. He guessed she'd been around NASCAR enough that she'd heard those words a few times. Still, sometimes he got so lost in the conversation that he forgot he was talking to a Christian woman and not his dad.

"I couldn't help bringing this to you," she said. "I hope you don't mind."

"No. I've been thinking about it all morning." He took the package and shook it. It was light. "Maybe Tyson just sent an empty package."

"You want to go get some lunch and open it?" she said.

He looked at the office staff. They pretended they were shuffling papers or expelling kids, but he knew they were watching. "Maybe I could just go for a walk?"

Mrs. Maxwell smiled. "Let's go."

She drove him to a park not far from the school, but it felt secluded. There were a bunch of tiny kids playing on playground in the distance with young moms pushing strollers and power walking around the paved track. Mrs. Maxwell left him there and went to get two subs from one of Tim's favorite restaurants. She already knew the kind of sandwich and all the toppings he liked by heart.

Tim sat at a picnic table and stared at the box. This thing sure had caused him a lot of trouble. But though he should have felt happy—at least that's what he thought he should feel like—he felt a little sad. He had discovered his father's stuff in a storage place back in Florida. He had talked with one of his dad's old friends (Charlie Hale, who drove the hauler), but this was the last link with his dad. Opening this would be the final piece of the puzzle—unless there was something else hidden out there.

He tore the paper around the box and immediately knew Tyson hadn't put this together. Probably somebody at the post office or one of those stores that send boxes in the mail. *How do those places stay in business?* he thought.

Tim ripped the tape from one side, sighed, then opened it. A gust of wind blew the packing peanuts all over the finely manicured grass and past the sign that said Please Help Keep Our Park Clean. He slammed the lid and chased them down until he had both pockets full. After he dumped them in the trash can, he retrieved a couple of strays near the duck pond. He imagined a duck choking on a packing peanut and people from some animal rights group throwing him in jail for "duck slaughter."

The package was waiting when he got back, and he opened only one end and stuck his hand inside. In the middle was something in bubble wrap. He pulled it out and found a picture frame. He undid the rubber bands and uncovered a wedding picture of his parents, both smiling. His mom was wearing a pretty dress—not one of those long, white ones you see in most weddings but just a flowery, blue dress. His dad had a suit on, and they were standing outside a brick building that looked more like a city office than a church.

He reached back inside and didn't find anything at first. Then, when he did a second sweep, he found a small square box at the back and pulled it out. Inside was a gold ring, too small to be his dad's. Plus a letter addressed to *Alexandra Carhardt* at a town in Florida he didn't recognize.

Lexy,

I pray that I get to give your ring back to you someday, but if you're reading this, that probably isn't going to happen. I've tried my best to take care of Timmy. He's such a good boy and I know he's missed you, but we've had fun on the road together. It almost hurts when I look at him and see you. He's the best of both of us that's for sure.

More than anything, I wish you could see the two of us together. I've given up the bad stuff, and I've actually found God. I know that's going to be hard for you to believe, but it's true. And every night I pray for you and wonder what you're doing and if you want to come back to us.

If you get this, know that I'm in a better place, not because I've made a lot of myself but because God's given me a great gift. I hope you find that peace for your life.

Don't blame yourself for anything. It's my fault what happened between us. I've loved you from the moment I met you and I still do. I always will.

With all my heart,
Martin

Tim held up the ring. He could barely get it on his little finger. Then he turned the letter over and studied the address. There was something familiar about it, like he'd seen it before but couldn't place it.

He opened the box again and looked for anything else in there. Nothing but those white peanuts.

He closed it, tossed it in the trash, and stuffed the ring and letter in his pocket and headed for the parking lot.

Mrs. Maxwell was there waiting with his sandwich. "You okay?"

Tim nodded. "Yeah. You can take me back to school."

JAMIE FLEW TO COLORADO on Friday evening, and her dad met her at the sprawling Denver airport. There had been rain earlier that day that washed out qualifying and they'd moved it to Saturday, so she and her dad had a nice meal at the new hotel that had been built near the track.

The altitude of Colorado made this one of the most interesting places to race in the country. Because it was a superspeedway, cars ran with a modified restrictor plate. It was modified because of the altitude. The first year of the race, just about every car on the track had trouble with vapor lock, basically an air bubble in the gas. And the altitude affected the downforce of the car—its ability to hug the track. But the people who built the Denver complex had done everything they could to make racing conditions for the cars and fans the best possible.

The track was a unique oval with severe banking and a track so wide that the cars could go four wide into the turns and never touch their brakes if they rode it correctly.

Denver had been one of Jamie's favorite venues to race on the simulator back at the school. She'd turned in the fastest qualifying lap, even faster than Chad. There was just something about the mountains in the background and the cooler air that sent a chill down her spine when she looked at the track and the surroundings.

As they ate, they planned Jamie's racing future. There were several venues where Jamie could still get her feet wet in the racing circle—though how she'd get a car was up in the air.

"A couple of our sponsors have approached me, saying they would be willing to put up some money," her dad said. "Maybe start small with some of the races in the east, then move up."

"Really?" Jamie said, dropping her fork. "That's awesome. How much have they offered?"

He told her, and she nearly spewed her Diet Mountain Dew on him.

"Just settle down," he said. "It's exciting to hear about that kind of money, but the responsibility can weigh on you. I'm going to talk with some guys around the track in the next couple of days to see if they know of any cars we could buy."

"I was talking with Tim today about going to college and racing at the same time. Do you think I could do that?"

He nodded. "I think that's a great plan. Ease into this while you get an education. Keep your options open."

"But I already know what I want to do," she said.

"Yeah, I can see it in your eyes."

She sighed and took a bite of her blackened chicken salad. "Your plan is better than Devalon's. He just wanted to throw me out there on the track and see what happened."

One of the TV commentators walked past and waved at them. Her dad offered a seat and the man sat down. "I'll only stay a minute, but I have to say, Jamie, that I watched the video of what you did at the school. Pretty impressive racing."

"Until the engine blew," she said. It was interesting hearing his voice right next to her instead of coming through the TV speakers. But he moved his hands and used the same expressions he did on the air.

"Yeah, but there are a lot of people talking about how you're at the top of the new wave of drivers," the man said. "Younger. Stronger. Better trained. Better athletes."

"Prettier too," her dad said.

The man laughed. "You got that right. I'm convinced the good old boy network is giving way to a new generation. More diverse, more open to different backgrounds—and especially females. We've had some really good women drivers, but nobody's had the chance to be the female wunderkind—the Tigress Woods, if you will."

Jamie laughed.

Her dad looked at her. "The Tigress has a ring to it, doesn't it?"

"I could paint the car with black stripes and wear a tail on my fire suit."

The commentator's eyes sparkled in the dim light. "I really believe you have what it takes, young lady. I've seen a lot of flashes in the pan, guys who looked promising but fizzled. You've got a good teacher here, so listen to him. I want to call your first win."

Jamie couldn't help smiling as the commentator got up and walked away. He stopped to shake hands with someone at another table. Butch Devalon.

"Oh, good grief," Jamie muttered.

"He's coming this way," her dad said.

Devalon strutted over to the table and pulled up his straight-legged jeans by his diamond-studded belt buckle, making sure they saw his championship ring on his right hand. He gave a little smile and nodded to both of them.

"I wanted to come over and apologize about what happened in Indy," Devalon said. "My son overheats like a bad engine, and he accused the boy living with you of some things. I wasn't a very good influence in the matter, and I want to tell you I'm sorry."

Jamie's dad looked at her like he'd just heard a dog sing "The Star-Spangled Banner." In French. While accompanying himself on the piano. "Well, that's nice of you to say, Butch. We both appreciate that."

"I wonder if you two would accept a ride tomorrow in my chopper over to the football stadium. Mile High something or other. I'm supposed to do a commercial shoot with a few of the players for one of the Monday Night Football games, and it'd be a treat to have you along."

"What about qualifying?" Jamie said.

"Oh, I'd have your dad back in plenty of time for that."

"Kellen would be drooling all over the table if he heard about it," her dad said.

Jamie kept her mouth closed. Butch Devalon was the last person she'd want to be seen with.

"That's nice of you, Butch, but I don't think—"

"One of your sponsors will be there. And there's

press covering it. We can use all the good press we can get—don't you think?"

"It was an olive branch," Jamie's dad said to her later as they were going up the elevator, the lights of Denver twinkling in the distance.

"It's not an olive branch. He's a snake with a stick. I'm surprised you don't see it."

"Won't hurt to go with him. Maybe he's a changed man. Plus, it'll take my mind off the qualifying. You and I both know I need a good spot to start from, and I have to finish well for any hope of getting into the Chase."

"I'll be at the track," she said.

LATE FRIDAY NIGHT Tim was watching a movie with Kellen, laughing at the antics of a silly-looking guy with long legs who did lots of stunts. There wasn't much to it except for him eating weird stuff or tripping over things, but it still had them rolling on the floor.

When it was over, Tim said, "If I had an address for a person and wanted to find out where that was, how would I do it?"

Kellen said he could go to a Web site and plug in the address, and it would show not only a map of the area but also a way to view the building with a satellite. "If the person you're looking for was playing basketball in the driveway when the satellite last took the picture, you could actually see them."

"Cool," Tim said. He went to his room, then came back upstairs when he was sure Kellen had gone to bed. He had talked to Mrs. Maxwell about the contents of the box, but he hadn't been specific about what the letter said.

He typed in the address and clicked the Search button. The computer worked a few seconds, as if it were teasing him. Then a screen popped up that said, "Several locations were found for this address. Please select one below."

He scrolled through the list, but only one matched. He clicked on it, and up came a listing for the Kathryn A. Ross Women's Correctional Facility.

Tim looked at the address on the envelope, then stared at the computer. He shook his head and turned the computer off.

JAMIE WENT TO THE TRACK and visited the team readying the car for qualifying. Her dad had left early for the meeting with Devalon. She'd heard the helicopter go overhead. Her dad's spotter, Scotty, walked through the hauler, eating an individually wrapped spice cake made by one of the sponsors. Jamie made a comment about him watching his weight.

Scotty frowned. "Easy for you to say. Everything I eat goes straight to my hips."

Jamie laughed. "You hear where my dad is?"

"He said he was going with Devalon somewhere. Hope he heard they moved qualifying up."

"To when?"

"First car rolls off in an hour. T.J.'s at the meeting now for the draw."

Chapter 42

Jamie dialed her dad, but he either had his phone off or wasn't taking calls. As much as it pained her, she walked over to the Devalon hauler and saw Chad's mom scurrying.

"Excuse me," Jamie said. "My dad is with your husband. Do you have his cell phone number?"

She looked up like a frightened squirrel. "I can't give that number to anyone. Butch would string me up if I did that."

"But I have to get in touch with my dad. They've moved qualifying up."

"Why don't you talk to his crew chief?" she said.

"He's at the draw now and . . ." Jamie hesitated as she saw Tad Renfro, one of the Devalon backup drivers, come out of the hauler with a fire suit on.

Devalon's crew chief walked up. "We got the 10th spot," he said to Tad. "Do your best."

Jamie hurried back to the Maxwell hauler as T.J. came in. "Hey, where's your dad?"

"He's with Devalon. Didn't he tell you?"

T.J.'s face turned white. "I got a call from Devalon's pilot that they canceled the shoot. I left a message on Dale's phone and at your room. He didn't get it?"

Jamie shook her head. "What did the pilot say?"

"Told me Dale was having breakfast with them and would be over for qualifying."

"Something's not right. Dad wouldn't do this. He

wouldn't cut it so close, especially with so much at stake. And I just saw Tad Renfro with a fire suit on."

"Renfro's going to qualify for Butch?" T.J. said, taking off his hat and scratching his head. "I think you're right. Something's fishy."

"Why would Devalon do this?"

"Your daddy's the strongest and hottest racer out there," T.J. said. "If Devalon can keep him out of the Chase, do you think he'd do it?"

"In a heartbeat."

He pulled a piece of paper from his pocket. "Your dad drew qualifying position number one. If he's going to make it, he's gotta get back here right now."

Jamie tried his cell again, but there was no answer. "Maybe we can call the football stadium."

"You work on it. I'll see what I can find out."

Jamie dialed home and got Kellen. He was on the computer and looking for a number at the stadium in seconds. Jamie got it, dialed, and got a voice mail. She listened to the options and chose an extension. Anybody who was alive would do.

"Hi, this is Rhonda and I'm not in the office right now, but if—"

Jamie punched the Star button to return to the tree and tried someone else.

After five tries a guy who sounded like he was bored answered. "This is Tony."

"Tony, are you at the stadium right now?"

"Yeah, I'm in the office. Who is this?"

Jamie told him. "My dad is supposed to be there with another guy shooting a commercial or something for Monday Night Football."

"Yeah, I heard they were here to do that—"

"I have to talk to him. It's an emergency."

"Let me transfer you to Shirley's cell—I think she's down there with them."

Please, God, Jamie prayed, *let me get through to him.*

The phone rang seven times before a harried woman answered. She seemed peeved.

"My dad is there with Butch Devalon. His name is Dale Maxwell—"

"Are you one of those NASCAR groupies trying to get an autograph?" she snapped.

"No. I'm his daughter, and he needs to get back to the track or he'll miss qualifying. Something's wrong with his phone, and I can't get through to him."

With an edge to her voice she said, "Hang on."

A second later Jamie heard, "Dale Maxwell."

"Dad, qualifying's about to start."

"What?" her dad yelled.

"I've been trying to reach your cell!"

He groaned. "It got turned off somehow."

"You have to get here quick."

"Butch told me qualifying was moved *back* an hour." There was a commotion behind them. Somebody shouted for quiet, but her dad spoke to Devalon. "You told me qualifying was moved back."

"No, I said it had been moved up," Devalon said in the background.

"Get your pilot out here now!" her dad hollered.

"Wouldn't make any difference," Devalon said. "We couldn't get you there in time if you have an early draw."

"What's my number?" her dad said to Jamie.

"You're first up."

Her dad muttered something through clenched teeth. It was the closest to cursing she'd ever heard. Then he spoke to Jamie. "Okay, listen. I'm in the race on owner points, but I don't want to start too low. I need your help."

"Dad, if the chopper can't get you here in time—"

"No, I can't make it. You'll have to get suited up and take the car out."

"Me?"

"Have T.J. walk you down to report. Show them your license and tell them about the situation."

"Driving a simulator is a lot different from—"

"Jamie, this is my only shot. I don't have another backup driver. Go out there and show them what you can do."

"What if I mess it up? ram into the wall or something?"

"I have every confidence in you. I'm not letting this guy shut me down, okay? You were right about him. Now let's turn this back against him."

JAMIE PUT ON her dad's fire suit, which hung on her like a tent. T.J. walked her to the NASCAR hauler and notified the officials that a backup driver would be qualifying for Dale. Jamie gave them her license, and there was a big discussion about it—she was sure it was because of her age. There had been talk in the past few years of lowering the age to 17, although some wanted it raised to 20.

Finally T.J., who was not one to mince words, said, "If she has a license, she's qualified. They waived that rule at the school. Now we're first up in qualifying, so we need to get moving."

The official eyed Jamie and pushed a clipboard toward her. "Sign here."

Outside the hauler she nearly threw up. She put on her helmet and ran to the pits, climbing into the car and strapping into her HANS device and the harness.

T.J. handed her the steering wheel. "Show 'em how to go fast out there."

Jamie pulled to the end of pit road and idled as an official stood glaring at her. Or maybe she was just imagining that. It could have been the face he used with every driver.

She didn't have her racing shoes or gloves, and her hands were sweating like crazy. Her stomach was in knots. She wished she could talk to her dad and tell him the seat was too big for her—that his rear was way too wide.

"Just relax and have fun," she imagined him saying. "Enjoy your first time qualifying."

THE TRACK RECORD, which was only two years old, was 186.44. Jamie tried to push that from her mind and go into her zone, but her HANS device suddenly felt like it was digging a hole in her neck. Behind her were the very racers she'd watched on TV every weekend of her life. She shook her head to clear it.

Focus, she told herself. *It's just a couple of runs around the track to see who can go fastest. I can do this.*

The official at the end of pit road put a hand to a headphone and nodded, saying something into the microphone.

She closed her eyes for a second, praying that the guy would not come over and tell her she'd have to get out of the car.

When she opened them, the guy gestured toward the track.

Jamie put the pedal down, roaring

past him. Picking up speed and shifting through the gears on the backstretch, she felt more comfortable. The car was solid and the engine hummed. As she took turn three, the massive incline felt just like the simulator. She shot out of turn four toward the green flag, flooring the accelerator.

The car felt like it was responding to every move. She drove low to the yellow line and inched up as she punched through. On the backstretch she really felt the speed and rode a bit higher in turns three and four, but when she passed the start/finish and got the white flag, she knew she'd had a good first lap.

"Good job. Now give me one more a little faster," T.J. said in her headset.

Her arms tense, her hands gripping the wheel until her knuckles were white, she flew around the turns.

"The Tigress is here, boys," she whispered to herself.

When she crossed the start/finish, she slowed a little into the turn and drove to the garage. T.J. was there to meet her, not saying a word about her time.

"How'd I do?" she said.

"Well, after one car, you've got the pole," he said.

"Funny," she said. "Seriously, how did I . . . ?" She took off her helmet and studied the scoring pylon. What she saw took her breath away.

CHRIS FABRY is a writer, broadcaster, and graduate of Richard Petty Driving Experience (top speed: 134.29 mph). He has written more than 50 books, including collaboration on the Left Behind: The Kids, Red Rock Mysteries, and the Wormling series.

You may have heard his voice on Focus on the Family, Moody Broadcasting, or Love Worth Finding. He has also written for *Adventures in Odyssey*, *Radio Theatre*, and *Kids Corner*.

Chris is a graduate of the W. Page Pitt School of Journalism at Marshall University in Huntington, West Virginia. He and his wife, Andrea, have nine children and live in Colorado.

If you'd like to get in touch with the author, you can reach him at chrisfabry@comcast.net.

RED ROCK MYSTERIES

BRYCE AND ASHLEY TIMBERLINE are normal 13-year-old twins, except for one thing—they discover action-packed mystery wherever they go. Wanting to get to the bottom of any mystery, these twins find themselves on a nonstop search for truth.

The Future Is Clear

Check out the exciting Left Behind: The Kids series